Playing for Pride

NATALIE FALKENWRATH

BENTON HOUSE PUBLISHING

Benton House Publishing

bentonhousepublishing.com

Copyright © 2022 Natalie Falkenwrath

ISBN 978-1-952057-09-0 (Paperback)

ISBN 978-1-952057-10-6 (eBook)

For more information about the author and

upcoming books, please visit

nataliefalkenwrath.com

Chapter 1
Morgan

Morgan VanDolen pulled her white Jeep into the dim cinderblock parking ramp and cut the engine. She looked at her watch. *Shit.* She was early—ridiculously early. It was a bad habit of hers, and although it was better than being late, she didn't like to waste time. *I could have gone home*, she realized. She didn't live far. Morgan had recently moved to an adorable little city— an older first-ring suburb with a small-town feel. She'd purposely picked a place within walking distance of its quaint but lively Main Street; there was no need to drive. But she had come straight from work, which was in the opposite direction, and she hated doubling back. It was inefficient. She took out her phone to pass the time with work tasks and social media. She was downtown to meet with her new softball team, the Dirt Bunnies.

When Morgan caught sight of her friend Kelly Seban's car pulling into the lot a few spots down, she quickly set aside her phone and hopped out of the Jeep.

This was the main reason Morgan had planned to be at least a little early: she wanted to walk in with Kelly. The Dirt Bunnies were Kelly's team; this was Morgan's first time meeting them, and she was uncharacteristically nervous.

"Hey, Morgan!" Kelly called out as the two came together. Kelly was wearing a Dirt Bunnies hoodie and jeans. A light breeze was blowing her jaw-length red hair into her face even as she attempted to tuck it behind her ears. "Punctual as ever, I see."

"Fifteen minutes early is on time, on time is late—" Morgan began.

"And late is unacceptable," Kelly finished, rolling her eyes. "Yeah, yeah."

The two walked together toward the neighborhood bar and grill, where they were meeting the team. Morgan wondered what Kelly would say if she knew that she'd been waiting in her car for nearly thirty minutes. *She'd probably think I was a nutcase. And she'd be right.*

"You told your team I've basically never played softball, right?" Morgan asked, wincing inwardly, embarrassed at her own trepidation. She must have asked Kelly that question a half-dozen times already. Kelly was her good friend and teammate–*hockey* teammate–Morgan had never felt insecure around her before. It was mortifying. And Kelly was clearly fed up with it.

"Yes, they know you haven't played softball," Kelly said with a huff. "Now, will you shut up about it? Anxiety doesn't suit you; it's weird. It's like, who are you, and what have you done with the cocky bitch we all know and love?"

"I think I left her at the rink." Morgan flipped her blonde braid back over her shoulder. "You know me from hockey, and you're the only one I know here, so I'm counting on you to give your team fair warning."

"Fair warning that you're a type-A competitive bitch?" Kelly teased.

"They just shouldn't expect much out of me; this isn't my sport, you know," Morgan replied, ignoring Kelly's comment. Being competitive was a point of pride for Morgan, even if it didn't always rub people the right way.

"Whatever, you're Morgan fucking VanDolen; you're an amazing athlete."

"I know I'm a great hockey player," Morgan said. There was no point in being humble. It was true, but it was also irrelevant. "But this isn't hockey, so I won't be one of the better players, and even if I'm not the *worst* player on the team, I don't like being near the bottom at all."

"Oh no. Poor Morgan doesn't get to be the best on the team for once." Kelly blew air out in a raspberry. "You'll live."

"We'll see." Morgan pulled open the door to the bar. There was no doubt that she was the was the best player on her hockey team. She'd even go so far as to say she was the best player in the whole division. She was confident and comfortable at hockey, but *softball?* Hockey and softball had very little in common. *If you made a Venn diagram of hockey and softball, hitting things with sticks would be just about the only thing in the middle*, Morgan thought to herself.

"I'm not the only one you know, by the way," Kelly said as they wound their way through the crowded bar.

Morgan snapped out of her thoughts. "What?"

"You've met Truck before, haven't you?" Kelly asked.

"Your girlfriend?"

"She's gonna be my wife soon," Kelly said with a grin.

"Oh yeah, I've met her. I keep forgetting she's on the team too." Morgan smirked and added *'lesbians'* to the center of her hockey-softball Venn diagram.

"Kelly!" A cherub-faced woman in a Minnesota Twins baseball cap waved excitedly from the center of the restaurant, where several high-top tables had been pulled together.

"Hey, Liz!" Kelly pulled out a chair opposite the woman and beckoned Morgan to sit beside her. "Liz, this is Morgan, the one I was telling you about from hockey. Morgan, this is Liz; she's our team manager."

"Nice to meet you." Morgan reached across the table and shook Liz's hand.

"Glad to have you with us, Morgan," Liz said with a cheerful squeak to her voice. "Kelly has told us so much about you. It's good to finally meet in person."

"She has, huh?" Morgan raised an eyebrow at Kelly.

"Mostly good things, I promise," Liz added with an oddly sharp giggle that sounded both cheerful and sinister at once. Kelly had told Morgan that Liz was a bit of a character. "Almost manically peppy." Morgan was starting to see what Kelly meant.

"'*Mostly* good.'" Morgan snorted. "Does that mean she's told you I'm new to softball or that I'm a… how did you put it, Kelly? 'Type-A competitive bitch?'"

Liz laughed again. "I like a little competitive spirit. Besides, she said you were athletic. She's sure you'll pick up the game quickly."

"I hope you're right," Morgan replied. "So tell me more about the team."

Liz and Kelly began filling Morgan in on the details about the upcoming season as more teammates continued to arrive. Morgan introduced herself to each in turn: Haley, Lindsey, Rebecca, and Jessica. Morgan was good with names when she paid attention to the people they identified. *Haley 'don't call me fish' Fischer, Lindsey the second-baseman, Rebecca the nearly silent one, and Jessica... she's a flirty thing, isn't she?* While Rebecca and Haley were both wearing Dirt Bunnies hoodies, Jessica was dressed in a tight purple top with a deep V-neck that showed off a considerable amount of cleavage. Morgan went through the names one more time in her head, committing them to memory.

When Kelly's girlfriend showed up, Morgan slid over a seat to let the two sit next to one another. They were an interesting pair. Kelly was built much like Morgan–tall and athletic, with broad shoulders, tight core, and a hockey player's solid quads and glutes. Truck, whose real name was Katie, could hardly have been more different. Short hair, short build–Truck was all curves over a strong, sturdy frame.

"What position do you play, Truck?" Morgan asked.

"Catcher."

"Oh, so Kelly pitches, and you catch?" Morgan raised a teasing eyebrow.

"Only on the diamond," Truck chuckled. "When we get home—"

"Shut up," Kelly whacked Truck, her face going pink.

Truck nuzzled closer to Kelly. "Come on, I thought you liked *Anton*," Truck said in a loud, throaty whisper.

"You know I do, but I don't think everybody else wants to hear about sex toys at the restaurant, babe," Kelly whispered back.

"Anton isn't just some toy; Anton's *my dick*, and he's awesome." Truck turned to wiggle her eyebrows at Morgan.

Kelly groaned and rolled her eyes. "For fuck's sake, Truck," she said. "Could you *not* traumatize our teammates?"

"I don't mind," Morgan said with a laugh, mostly to tease Kelly, who threw her head back in an exasperated sigh.

"Neither do I. I'd love to swap strap-on stories some time," Jessica chimed in with a mischievous smile on her pouty lips.

"Don't scare off the straight girls," Liz tisked.

"I dare you to try," Lindsey said with a snort.

Morgan chuckled as she eyed Rebecca, Jessica, and Haley, trying to read these new faces and wondering which of them were part of the aforementioned 'straight girls.' Morgan had been *painfully* single lately. That softball might be a new avenue to meet some available ladies was a bonus.

Rebecca and Jessica were attractive, albeit different; Rebecca had a simple farm-girl charm and Jessica was a total bombshell. But Haley was a bit asymmetrical and awkward. Morgan could see asking Rebecca out. She figured she'd have a good chance of getting a yes—assuming she was gay and single. And assuming Morgan didn't embarrass herself too much on the field.

Morgan couldn't discount the chance that this could be a one-and-done situation. If Liz was a competitive team manager, would she really put up with a total newbie? Morgan wouldn't have tolerated it on her hockey team. *Maybe that just makes me an asshole.* She was comfortable being a little bit of an asshole if it meant her team would win. Was it hypocritical to hope Liz wouldn't be the same way?

"Sorry I'm late, guys." A voice behind Morgan's right ear cut through her thoughts, prompting her to turn. When she did, the air caught in her lungs. *Oh, wow.* Before her stood a petite, beautiful woman with dark brown eyes, curly hair that shone like polished mahogany under the bar lights, and the most alluring Mona Lisa smile. Morgan had never felt so quickly entranced. *This one. This is the one I want.*

"Well, you wouldn't be you if you weren't late," Liz said, although Morgan barely heard her. She was lost in this woman's face. The curve of her cheek, the freckles that dotted her nose. She was *perfect.*

"Come on, pull up a seat and meet our new recruit, Morgan," Jessica patted the seat beside herself.

Morgan started at the mention of her name. Although she still couldn't peel her eyes from the woman's face, she did manage to find her voice. "Hello, I'm Morgan VanDolen," she said, a bit too loudly, extending her hand. *Why am I being so formal? I sound like I'm at work.* Morgan wasn't used to being so thrown by the sight of a pretty woman. All she could do was look into those dark, alluring eyes and try to remember to breathe. Marina tilted her head slightly, her smile growing ever so faintly.

"Hello, Morgan VanDolen," the woman said, taking her hand. "I'm Marina."

"It's good to meet you, Marina," Morgan said, unable to stop looking at the beautiful woman's face, even after their handshake had dropped. Marina turned and walked around the table, past her teammates, to the open seat beside Jessica.

Marina settled into a seat and cleared her throat. "Are we getting food? Did you guys order?" she asked, her gaze wandering across the group at large. She caught Morgan's eye, and Morgan blinked—suddenly realizing she'd been staring. *Act natural, VanDolen. You've seen a pretty girl before.*

"Just drinks," Morgan answered. She turned to Kelly. "Do you normally get food?" It was hard to turn away from Marina, but she didn't want to get caught staring again.

"Not always," Kelly said. "But to be fair, most of our team 'events' are out in the parking lot at the ballpark. More of a 'chips and beer' kind of thing."

"I'm gonna get real food today, though," Truck chimed in. "I'm starving, and something in here smells amazing."

"I bet that's the fajitas," Kelly offered.

Morgan sniffed. There was the faint but distinct scent of grilled onions. Her stomach rumbled. "Well, I'm starving," she said, reaching across the table for a menu. "Let's order."

Chapter 2
Marina

Marina Martin glanced down the table at her new teammate. The woman had been staring at her on-and-off all evening. It was slightly disconcerting—she had the most piercing blue eyes. Something about Morgan's gaze made butterflies flutter in Marina's stomach.

She is very attractive. Morgan's face was remarkably beautiful in a bold sort of way. She had high cheekbones, a long straight nose, strong jaw, and flawless complexation. Her long blonde hair was worn in a braid down her back, and although Morgan was seated, Marina could tell she was tall. *She looks like a pro athlete,* Marina thought, *that or a model.* Morgan carried herself with the confidence of a model. Marina envied that; she wished she could go into new situations with such poise.

Marina was at home amongst the Dirt Bunnies—she'd been playing with them for years—but Morgan seemed able to jump into the group as if she automatically belonged. Marina knew she couldn't have done the same if the roles were reversed. Marina wasn't a complete introvert, but it took her time to get used to people enough to relax around them. *Morgan is already friends with Kelly; that's probably why she's so chill.*

Marina glanced around the table. She was comfortable with her team, but she wouldn't say she was particularly close friends with any of them. *I'm kind of friends with Jessica.* They had fun together during the season. But Marina didn't hang out with her—or anyone really. She had a boyfriend, Jason, and she spent time with him and his buddies, but aside from that she didn't really have her own friends—just acquaintances from work and softball. *Maybe I should try and get closer with my teammates.*

Some of her teammates were obviously already close. Two of them were even dating. *I wonder if Morgan is dating anybody.* Marina had the thought without really knowing why. It's not as if she were available herself; she was in a serious relationship. Besides which, she didn't even know if Morgan liked women. Despite being bi, Marina had absolutely no "gaydar"—if that was even a real thing. *What does it matter to me if Morgan's gay?* It wasn't as if Morgan would be interested in *her*. Girls never seemed interested in her at all. And certainly not ones as gorgeous and confident as Morgan.

At that moment, Morgan glanced her way—as if she could hear Marina's thoughts. She smiled at Marina in a way that made Marina's cheeks flush hot. She quickly looked away, fixing her attention on Jessica. "What's new with you these days, Jessica?"

Jessica was a pretty little thing, with the curves of a pinup girl and plump, pouty lips. In another context, Marina might have been intimidated by her looks—as she was with Morgan—but Jessica was so friendly and easy to talk to. Besides which, she was one of the Dirt Bunnies' worst players, and somehow that made her more approachable. *She's the closest thing I have to a friend on the team; maybe I should try to get closer to her.*

"Not much new." Jessica shrugged. "I'm in a bit of a rut. I need some fresh excitement in my life."

"Does the start of the softball season count as excitement?" Marina asked.

"Not unless—hey, are people leaving already?"

Marina looked down the table. Sure enough, the server was handing out checks, and their teammates looked ready to split. "Seems like it."

"That stinks," Jessica pouted. She and Marina followed suit, paying their tabs along with the others. "Want to stick around a little longer?" Jessica asked.

"Sure, I guess," Marina agreed. *Maybe Jessica and I are closer friends than I thought if she wants to hang out with me after the team leaves.* Marina smiled.

"Cool, wait here," Jessica said, walking off toward the bar. Marina watched her slip onto a barstool next to one of the men sitting there.

Or maybe not? Am I just holding the table for her? Marina grumbled internally as she bade her other teammates farewell, awkwardly explaining that she was waiting for Jessica.

"It was good to meet you," Morgan said as she moved to go. She was looking so directly into Marina's eyes with such focused intensity it was as if she were looking right into her mind.

"Good, yeah, you too," Marina stammered.

Morgan grinned. "See you on the field, Marina." She winked at Marina, and Marina felt heat rise in her cheeks. *Is she flirting with me?* She knew there was nothing she could *do* about it if Morgan were. But all the same, the attention made her body tingle.

I hope she's a good softball player. Marina had seen many women come and go on the Dirt Bunnies, but she found herself hoping that Morgan would stick around.

"Yeah, see you." Marina managed before Morgan turned and strode out of the bar. Just as the door closed behind Morgan, Jessica sauntered back to the table, a mischievous smile curling her lips and a drink in each hand. She set one in front of Marina.

"Why do you look like a cat that just caught a mouse?" Marina asked as Jessica settled back into her seat across the table.

Jessica's smile widened, and she waved a cocktail napkin at Marina before turning back to blow a flirty kiss in the direction of the bar. Marina looked up in time to see a man point and wink at Jessica.

"What's with that?" Marina asked.

Jessica tossed the napkin on the table with a casual flick of her wrist. "Oh, that guy just bought us these drinks. I wouldn't give him my number, but I let him give me his." She sighed. "I probably won't call, but he seemed a little desperate, and I always like having a sure thing in my back pocket—a back-pocket penis, if you will—just in case."

"Back-pocket penis?" Marina squinted at her. "In case of what?"

"In case I desperately need to *get some*," Jessica said, pulling back her shoulders and thrusting her chest forward in a suggestive manner.

"Huh?" Marina was a bit lost.

Jessica shrugged. "If I'm in the mood to fuck a dude, it might be him."

"But I thought you had a girlfriend," Marina replied, still confused.

"Sure, but I don't have a *boyfriend*." Jessica laughed. "Not that I couldn't do with some back-pocket-pussy too. You know, for when Cassie's *busy*." Jessica must have seen continued confusion on Marina's face because she laughed again. "My girlfriend and I are non-monogamous," she explained. "She's my only serious relationship, but we both sleep with other people."

Marina had heard of non-monogamy before, but she'd never really understood it. "How does that work? If you don't mind me asking."

"Oh, not at all!" Jessica said. "We're just both kind of… slutty."

"But you're dating?"

"Yup. I love her, and she loves me, and we both love sex. It's just that sometimes that sex is with other people." Jessica said this so casually.

"Don't you get jealous?" Marina asked quietly. She felt like she was prying, but at the same time, Jessica was such an open person, and Marina was genuinely curious.

"If she lands a super hottie, sometimes I get jealous *of* her. But no, not when it's just sex." Jessica tapped her index finger on her chin. "If somebody ever tried to break us up, or get in between us emotionally, then I might cut a bitch. Or dude. Whatever. I guess I could be jealous that way."

"But that has never happened?" Marina asked.

"Nope. And I don't see it happening." Jessica snorted. "Not with Cassie."

"What do you mean by that?"

"I mean, our relationship is special. I just don't see anybody ever getting between us." Jessica said. "You know, for a long time, Cassie honestly didn't think she ever would really fall in love. It took a fair amount of convincing to get her to admit she had feelings for me beyond the bedroom." Jessica's eyes were suddenly unfocused as if she were seeing something—or someone—that wasn't there. She smiled a soft dreamy smile. "But she loves me. And that makes me the luckiest bitch in the world."

It didn't make much sense to Marina. *How can she so clearly be in love but still be okay sleeping with other people?* "I don't really get it, to be honest. But if you're happy, more power to you."

Jessica blinked, snapping herself out of her doe-eyed swooning over her girlfriend. "Most people don't get it. Hell, people can't even get their simple minds around the idea of being attracted to more than one *gender,* much less more than one person. But that's who we are: bi unicorns in love." She laughed. "Rumor has it you're bi too," she added, wiggling her eyebrows at Marina.

"Uh, I, yeah, but—" Marina began.

"Oh, don't worry, I don't think you're slutty because you're bi. I'm slutty because I'm slutty, sexuality completely aside." She flicked her wrist, dismissing the ridiculous—if common—notion that being bi is what made her "slutty." "What I wanted to ask you—which you don't have to answer, I know it's like the total *cliché* question. I'm just curious. I'm like a teenager playing truth or dare twenty-four-seven…"

"Curious about what?" Marina asked.

"If you've slept with women before."

The question hit Marina hard, her stomach dropping as if she'd just swallowed a lead weight, and she could feel her cheeks immediately begin to burn. "I… uh…" She looked at her lap.

"Oh, sweety. I'm sorry I brought it up if it's a sensitive topic," Jessica said, her voice soft. "There's nothing to be embarrassed about if you haven't, you know. It took me a long time to really fuck a girl, myself. And I'm a total ho-bag."

Marina laughed softly. "No, I… I don't have a lot of experience with girls."

Jessica leaned forward and patted Marina's hand; her green eyes seemed to reflect genuine understanding. "Girls can seem complicated and scary at first," she said. "Men are *so* easy by comparison. At least when it comes to getting them into bed."

"You're not wrong," Marina agreed, feeling herself relax. Knowing that somebody as confident as Jessica could have ever found women scary was somewhat of a comfort. "I had opportunities with girls. But I was never brave enough to, you know, make a move."

"Opportunities?" Jessica leaned forward conspiratorially. "Do tell."

Marina looked at her drink and sighed. These weren't stories that were always easy to tell, but it was just her and Jessica there at the table. "Well," she began.

"There was one time I somehow ended up making out with this girl at a dance club—"

"Ooh, that's how Cassie and I met," Jessica snickered. "But I take it you didn't end up doing it in the DJ booth?"

Marina shook her head. "Not even close. We didn't get past some handsy kissing. But she did give me her number and told me where she was staying—she was only in town for the weekend—but I never followed up." Marina winced slightly at the memory. Not only because she wished she'd done things differently, but because she knew if it happened again, she still would never have the guts to have called. "I'm such chicken shit. It makes me wonder if I really even want to sleep with a woman. If I can't get up the guts—"

"Hey, rando hook-ups aren't for everybody," Jessica assured her. "That doesn't mean you didn't *want* to sleep with her."

"Yeah, I know…" Marina twisted her fingers. "It still bugs me. But the ones that really get to me are the, like missed connections in real life."

"Such as?" Jessica coaxed.

Marina sighed in wistful remembrance. "There was a time I found out, after the fact, that a good friend of mine, Vanessa, had liked me. I liked her too—so much more than the guy I was dating at the time. But I had no idea she felt that way. If I'd known…" Marina's throat caught; telling the story was bringing up more emotion than she'd expected. "By the time I found out, she'd moved away. We're still Facebook friends, but we never really got a real chance…" Marina swallowed hard. It wouldn't do to get all teary-eyed here at the bar.

"Hey, it's okay," Jessica said, reaching over to squeeze Marina's hand. "Life is too short to worry about what-ifs and if-onlys."

"Easier said than done." Marina didn't think she'd ever really get over Vanessa and the missed chances she represented. But sharing with Jessica felt cathartic. She was glad she'd decided to try to get closer with her teammate. "Thanks for listening," Marina said.

"Anytime, lady. What are friends for?"

Chapter 3
Morgan

The first game of the Dirt Bunnies' season took place on a hot, sunny day at the ballpark a few blocks from Morgan's house in the center of the residential part of town. The park was nicely designed—two diamonds with a small pavilion in between that housed concessions and bathrooms. The fields were well-kept, but it hadn't rained in a while, and the slightest motion kicked up clouds of dust which stuck to the sweat on Morgan's face and neck. However, Morgan wasn't concerned about getting dirty; she was worried about *failing*. She tried to stay focused and optimistic, but she was itching with frustration by the second inning.

"Strike two!" the umpire shouted, and Morgan swallowed a curse. *How the hell am I striking out? I'm better than this,* she admonished herself silently. Sure, softball wasn't really her sport, but Morgan expected more. She was a *hockey player*. If she didn't miss passes from a speeding puck, how was she missing a slow-pitched *softball*? It defied logic. Morgan tightened her grip on the bat.

The pitcher let the ball fly, and Morgan swung again. This time she made contact. The ball struck with a loud crack that sent the ball hurling back in the direction of the pitcher, who caught it easily.

"Out!"

"God fucking dammit." Morgan retreated to the bunch, muttering curses. "I told you that you might regret letting me on your team," she grumbled, dropping down next to Kelly.

"Oh whatever," Kelly rolled her eyes. "You made contact, didn't you?"

"Fat load of good that does if I hit it right to their player," Morgan huffed. She peered down the row at the other players. If they were upset with her performance, they didn't show it. *Chill out, VanDolen,* she scolded herself. *It's beer-league softball. You warned them that you suck. There's no reason for them to be disappointed.* But Morgan couldn't help how she felt. She'd failed to get on base, and failing wasn't something she tolerated in herself.

Liz was next up to bat. She hit the first pitch, sending the ball over the pitcher's head. It bounced on the grass in the outfield a few times before the other team scooped it up, earning Liz a spot on first base. The other Dirt Bunnies clapped and cheered. Morgan should have been happy for her team. But all she felt was bitterness over how easy Liz made it look. *She doesn't even seem athletic*, Morgan thought as she watched Liz panting from the short run to first.

"Stop comparing yourself," Kelly said, elbowing Morgan in the ribs. "She's our best hitter."

"You know me too well." Morgan shot Kelly a half-smile.

"Yeah, and that's why I know you need to settle down. It's the first game. You'll get into the *swing* of it." Kelly grinned, showing off her crooked teeth.

"That was bad," Morgan groaned. She turned her eyes back to the game; Truck was up to bat. She fouled the first pitch and missed the second. She hit the third, but it was a pop fly that the outfielder easily caught, ending the inning.

"See, she didn't do any better than you, and she's played softball for *years*," Kelly said as the team prepared to move to fielding.

Truck gave her a playful shove. "Hey now. Don't be comparing me to Morgan, woman." She crossed her arms and narrowed her eyes at Kelly. "Or maybe *Anton* won't want to come out to play tonight."

"You're bringing *Anton* into this?" Kelly said with a pout. When Truck didn't budge, Kelly scoffed. "Oh, come on, you know you're better than Morgan. We wouldn't trust her as catcher, would we?"

Truck grinned. "Okay, threat revoked." She kissed Kelly on the cheek before pulling on her catcher's mask.

"No offense," Kelly said to Morgan.

Morgan waved dismissively at her as she picked up her glove. "None taken. I'm shocked you trust me with anything in the infield, honestly." The team had put her on first base—a decision that seemed stupidly risky given her lack of experience.

"You're fast, and you can catch," Kelly said with a shrug. "Besides, you can't throw for shit over long distances, so it's not like we could put you in the outfield."

"I suppose," Morgan grumbled.

"Hey, I'm just fucking with you. Come on, have some fun." Kelly trotted off to the pitcher's mound, and Morgan took her spot at first. She glanced down the baseline. Marina was smiling brightly and chatting with Lindsey as she took her position between second and third base. Her soft curls were tied back in a ponytail that stuck out from the back of her blue baseball cap; she was wearing black leggings and a thin black tank top over a purple sports bra. She was just as captivating today as she'd been the first time Morgan had laid eyes on her. But this was no time for admiring pretty women. Morgan turned away and punched her fist into her glove. She needed to focus on the game. Although she was usually decent at catching, she'd missed an easy throw in the first inning, resulting in a player getting on base, and she didn't want to repeat that mistake.

Kelly kicked at the dirt on the pitcher's mound before winding up to throw. If you could call it winding up. Morgan still didn't fully understand how the pitching portion of slow pitch worked. She'd watched a bunch of college softball online to prepare for the season, but fast-pitch and slow-pitch seemed almost unrelated to her untrained eye. Fast-pitch was so much more intense; that was part of what made striking out here so painfully embarrassing. It was just so *slow*. Morgan sighed. *It's a good thing it's slow. I wouldn't stand a damn chance otherwise.*

Kelly let the ball fly, and it landed with a thud in Truck's glove—the first in a series of strikes that gave the team their first out. Each time Kelly wound up, Morgan held her breath in anticipation of what might happen. It felt sort of like a face-off in a hockey game—waiting for the puck to drop, not knowing until the split second it happened who would win the draw. But at hockey, Morgan was the one that took the face-offs—and won them. The tension was exciting; it was the best part of fielding.

The game ended with the Dirt Bunnies winning a narrow two-run victory. The rest of the team whooped and cheered, but Morgan was quiet and contemplative as they filed off the field. Objectively, she knew she had made more good plays than mistakes. She even got on base in the sixth inning. But every strike, every off-target throw, every dropped ball haunted her. And the more she reflected on the game, the more frustrated she grew.

"I played like such shit. Did you see that time I *batted the ball down* rather than catch it?" Morgan grumbled to Kelly as they picked up their gear.

"Oh, would you shut up," Kelly scoffed. "We won, didn't we?

"Barely."

"Perk the fuck up and let's go get a beer," she said, pushing Morgan in the direction of the parking lot. The team was already congregating around a dusty red Honda—Liz's car.

Morgan took a deep breath. The sun was finally starting to dip below the trees, but the air was still warm, her skin still damp with sweat. She wiped her sleeve across her face. "Yeah, I suppose I could go for a cold one."

When they got to the car, Liz handed them drinks. Kelly took hers, leaned against the bumper, and struck up a conversation with Liz. *I think Kelly's had enough of me for one day.* Morgan took a beer, cracked it open, and looked around. Marina was standing quietly, sipping her drink and listening to the chatter around her. Morgan took a deep breath and stepped up to the curly-haired beauty.

"Hey, Marina,"

"Oh, hi, Morgan," Marina replied, turning so that she was looking directly at her.

"You remembered my name," Morgan said.

"Well, you are pretty memorable," Marina said.

Morgan's heartbeat ticked up a notch. *I'm noticeable? In a good way? Is she flirting? Or was it my terrible playing?* "Because I'm so bad?" She asked with what she hoped was a relaxed expression.

"What? Oh, no. Just because you're new to the team, I mean," Marina amended.

"Oh, duh," Morgan said, slapping herself on the forehead. There was an awkward pause. *Come on, VanDolen. Talk to the pretty girl without being a total moron.* "So, you play shortstop, huh?" Morgan asked.

"Yeah," Marina said simply.

"Well, you are short," Morgan teased, grinning at her. She couldn't read Marina's expression and rushed to add, "and quick. Perfect for a shortstop. You seem good at it anyway." She didn't know if that was true; shortstop was the position she knew the least about. Morgan made a mental note to watch more softball videos focused on shortstops.

"Thanks, I guess," Marina said, giving Morgan one of her soft smiles. "Did you enjoy your first game?"

Morgan considered the question seriously. Despite being frustrated with herself, she *had* enjoyed the challenge. At least a little. Slowly Morgan nodded. "Yes," she said, "but I would enjoy it more if I didn't suck so much." She grinned, trying to project confidence through her self-deprecation.

"I thought you did fine," Marina said.

Morgan shook her head. "Fine" wasn't acceptable. Not for a VanDolen. "I can do better."

"If you say so," Marina said. She chewed her lip a moment before asking, "Do you normally play first base?"

"Well, I don't *normally* play anything," Morgan replied. "Or I should say, I normally play *hockey*."

"Ice hockey?" Marina asked.

"Yup," Morgan grinned. "It's pretty much my life."

"That's cool."

"I play with her too," Kelly said, suddenly stepping in to join the conversation. She threw her arm around Morgan. "Not that it matters that I'm even there," she added with a smirk.

"It matters," Morgan said, shrugging her off. She wished she could have continued the conversation with Marina alone. Marina's big brown eyes were still steadily trained on her, that alluring little smile on her lips. But as much as Morgan wanted to, she couldn't just *ignore* Kelly. "You lead the team in assists," she said.

Kelly rolled her eyes. "That's just because I pass to you," she countered.

Morgan let out a bark of laughter. "True," she said. "But still, you're the *best* at passing to me. I wish all my wings were like you."

"You're that good?" Marina asked.

Morgan grinned. "Sure am." Beside her, Kelly rolled her eyes again, and Morgan laughed. "But the roles are reversed now, aren't they?" she said. "So, what's the softball equivalent of an assist?" Passing you the ball?"

"Sure, I guess. 'Pass' the right person the ball, anyway," Kelly replied.

Morgan considered this. "I'll have to work on the speed and accuracy of my throws. You guys don't practice as a team, do you?"

"Hell no," Kelly said with a derisive snort.

"But I could help you," Marina offered, unexpectedly. "If you want, that is."

Is she blushing? Morgan couldn't help but wonder if Marina was flirting with her a little. *It couldn't hurt to flirt back.* "I'd love that." Morgan winked at Marina. "Then I know I'll get better for sure."

Marina's blush deepened. "Um, uh, good. We'll have to set it up some time."

This definitely felt like a flirty moment. "Give me your phone," Morgan said. "I'll put my number in."

Silently Marina handed it over.

Morgan entered her number and sent herself a text. "There, now we're connected," she said, looking into Marina's endlessly beautiful face.

"You're both on the team text chain, you know," Kelly cut in.

"Yeah, but I want to make sure I know which one is Marina, specifically," Morgan replied, not taking her eyes off Marina. Marina looked back at her, and Morgan could swear she felt electricity spark between them. But if it was there, it only lasted a moment.

"I, uh, I should be going home," Marina said suddenly. She turned to Kelly. "Good game, Kelly."

"You too," Kelly replied.

"I'll see you both at the next game," Marina said as she turned to go.

"I'll be there," Morgan replied. *I wouldn't want to be anywhere else.*

Chapter 4
Marina

A few hours before the Dirt Bunnies were scheduled to play their second game of the season, Marina received a text from Liz. "Today's game is canceled. Sorry for the short notice but I guess the other team didn't have enough players."

Well, that sucks. Marina was sitting on the yellow and brown patterned sofa in her living room, watching TV with her boyfriend, Jason. They'd been like this all morning; she'd been looking forward to the game. Marina barely had time to process her disappointment when her phone went off again.

"Do we still have the field reserved? Could we use the time to practice? Since we were planning on being there anyway it seems like a good opportunity." The text came from Morgan. Marina smiled to herself. *She is an intense one, isn't she?* Marina liked it.

"I told you we don't usually practice," Kelly responded.

Marina typed out a text. "I think it's a good idea." She *had* offered to help Morgan practice, after all. *And that wink...* "I'll plan to head over in any case," she added.

"Great!!!" Morgan replied.

"Well, I do already have the beer. I guess it couldn't hurt to get in a little bit of 'practice,'" Liz responded, adding a winking emoji to the end of the text. The Dirt Bunnies had never practiced before, and Marina highly doubted that much ball play would go on before the first drink was cracked open. Still, she liked the idea of hanging out with her team. *And Morgan.* Marina got a little light-headed when she thought of her. She'd looked so inexplicably sexy at their game last week. Red-faced and sweating, her eyes concentrated on the play during the game and on *her* afterward. Marina shivered.

"What's going on?" Jason asked. "You've got a funny look on your face."

"Oh, softball stuff," Marina said dismissively, feeling suddenly guilty for thinking about Morgan like that while sitting next to Jason. *Why should I feel weird about that? It's not like I'm ever going to do anything with Morgan. She's eye-candy at best.* Jason knew

Marina was bi; he liked that she appreciated attractive women—it was a turn-on for him. If she did tell him about Morgan—about her long legs, subtle curves, and perfect skin—he'd be thrilled. He'd probably even go with her to get a look at the new hottie for himself.

"The game was canceled, but the team is still getting together," Marina said, setting down her phone and sliding closer to her boyfriend. "In theory, it's going to be a practice, but I'd bet we hit a few balls, call it good and then sit around drinking."

"That sounds like a good time," Jason replied, putting his arm around Marina and pulling her close. She looked up at him—at his dark, disheveled hair and deep blue eyes. She put a hand on his cheek and stroked his facial hair; it always lingered somewhere between a five o'clock shadow and a short beard. She liked it like that. She kissed him, and his near-beard scratched her face in that familiar way that she both loved and hated. *Girls' faces are always so smooth.* Everything about women seemed soft and smooth compared to men. *Kissing Morgan would feel so different.*

Marina pulled back. *Where did* that *come from?* Marina often noticed pretty girls, but she didn't usually envision kissing them. Now she felt *really* guilty for thinking about Morgan while with Jason. "Hey, do you want to sneak in a quicky before I have to leave?" she asked.

Jason grinned. "Have I ever said no to an offer like that?"

Marina pulled off her shirt. "No, and I hope you never do," she purred, climbing onto his lap.

Their "quicky" went a bit longer than Marina had anticipated. *I should have known that would happen.* She jumped up when they were done. She rushed out of the house, leaving Jason smiling sleepily behind her.

She arrived at the baseball field more than fifteen minutes late. To her surprise, when she got there, the team was actually practicing. Most of the players looked tired and bored. Rebecca was yawning in the outfield, Lindsey was kicking lazily at the dirt, and Liz was standing, hands on her hips, an exasperated expression on her normally cheerful face. Everybody looked completely over it. Everybody but Morgan. She was crouched in a ready position, waiting for Truck to hit the ball, her eyes narrowed in concentration.

"What's going on?" Marina asked Jessica, who was on the other side of the fencing behind home plate, poking at her phone.

Jessica pocketed the phone. "'*Practice*,'" she said, making air quotes with her fingers. Jessica didn't look dressed for softball at all. She was wearing skin-tight jeans and a tank top cut so low her breasts would surely fall out if she tried to run. But she had her glove, and she was there. "You're late as always, I see," Jessica teased.

"You're dressed inappropriately as always, I see," Marina teased back.

Jessica laughed. "I didn't actually expect we'd *do* anything. Plus, Cassie is meeting me here later, and I gotta look bangable." She looked Marina up and down and narrowed her eyes. "Speaking of, you're late because you were having sex, aren't you?"

"Is it that obvious?" Marina laughed and touched the back of her head. *Do I have noticeable sex hair?* She hadn't had time to comb it out, but she had pulled it back into a ponytail.

Jessica laughed again. "No, not to most people. I've got sex-magic-vision," she said. "So, was it good?"

"I wouldn't be late if it wasn't," Marina said with a little smile. It had been good. She may not have been quite the horn-dog Jessica was, but she did enjoy sex.

"Nice," Jessica nodded in approval. "I plan to score soon myself."

"Yeah, you mentioned," Marina said. "But are you ever going to score a *run* this season?"

Jessica blew a raspberry at her. "Har har." She nodded toward the diamond; the team had shifted to new positions while they were talking. "Bet I get more runs than the new chick," Jessica whispered.

Morgan was standing at home, holding the bat in a death grip as she swung at—and missed—pitch after pitch. *She really could use practice*, Marina mused.

Morgan muttered something under her breath as another ball made it past her un-hit. She was clearly tense. Marina could see frustration radiating off her, even at a distance. It probably didn't help that Kelly was *clearly* sick of pitching.

"Hey, don't worry, Morgan. It wasn't a great pitch anyway," Truck said as she tossed the ball back to Kelly.

"I heard that!" Kelly called out from the pitcher's mound.

"I just call 'em like I see 'em, babe," Truck shouted back with a chuckle. Marina smiled. Truck and Kelly were such a fun couple. They brought a lot of laughter to the team with their back-and-forth banter.

"Seriously, girl, relax." Truck smacked Morgan on the ass with the back of her glove.

"I don't want to relax," Morgan growled. "I want to hit the goddamned ball." She rolled her shoulders and then stepped into place again. Kelly tossed the ball. This time Morgan made contact, hitting a line drive that whizzed past the players and bounced along the grass of the outfield where Rebecca jogged languidly to retrieve it. It was a good hit, but Morgan still didn't look satisfied.

"See, that's the Morgan I know; that's the lady whose slapshots leave welts the size of softballs," Kelly shouted with a laugh.

"Fat load of good it'll do in a game if it takes four pitches." Morgan wiped her face with the bottom of her t-shirt, briefly exposing her flat, toned stomach. *Damn, she's in shape*, Marina thought, admiring the view. *But why does she look so tired?* Marina hadn't been at the field for long, but the practice hadn't seemed particularly rigorous from what she had seen. Nobody else had broken a sweat, and yet Morgan was red-faced with apparent exertion.

"You're too hard on yourself," Liz called from first base.

"I'm just figuring out what I need to work on. I don't like to suck," Morgan replied.

"You don't suck." Liz shook her head. "Don't be negative."

"I'm not being negative. I'm being accurate," Morgan insisted. "I'm reasonably good at catching. I'm not perfect, but I've got good reflexes, and I'm fast. Overall, I'm… sporty."

"And modest," Truck laughed. Marina snickered.

"I'm not saying it to brag; I'm just making the point that I know my own strengths and therefore also see my weaknesses," Morgan said seriously. "I'm terrible at long throws, and my batting average is fucking atrocious. I'll improve if I practice, but in the meantime, I'm going to get mad at myself when I screw up. That's just how I am."

"Yeah, well, try to keep your frustration to yourself," Liz said, a hint of animosity in her voice. Morgan was getting under her skin; Marina could see it. Liz began to walk toward Morgan. "This is supposed to be fun. Alright?"

"Yeah, but don't you care about winning?" Morgan squinted at her.

"I do care about winning, but I like my team to stay positive, okay?" Liz said with forced cheer.

Morgan smiled thinly back at her. "Okay, sorry," she replied, although she still looked frustrated.

Liz put her fingers in her mouth and whistled. "That's it for today," she called out. The players began to meander back from the field toward where Marina and Jessica were standing.

Morgan didn't move with the others. "Oh, come on, just a few more pitches?" she pleaded to Kelly as the team filed past her.

Kelly pulled off her glove. "No thanks, my arm's tired, and my belly is in dire need of beer," she said, nodding in the direction of the parking lot.

"But I really do need more practice," Morgan protested, "and I can't do that without a pitcher."

"Drop it, VanDolen. Practice is over; come have a drink." Truck put an arm around Kelly's waist, and they both began to walk off the park. Marina didn't move. She watched Morgan roll her shoulders—clearly agitated.

"Not much of a practice," Morgan huffed.

It's a new sport for her. She just wants to improve. Not that Marina didn't also understand Liz's perspective; practicing wasn't really something the Dirt

Bunnies did. But Marina wanted to help. She stepped around the fence, coming up behind Morgan.

"I could toss you a few," she said. Morgan turned, her bright eyes landing on Marina with surprise like she hadn't even realized Marina had been there. Marina smiled. "If you want to keep practicing," she added.

"Oh, hey, yeah, thanks," Morgan said, sounding confused.

"Something wrong?" Marina asked, made unsure by Morgan's curious reaction.

"What? No. Sorry, I guess I was so focused I didn't see you were here."

Marina waved dismissively. "I was really late. I practically just arrived."

The confusion on Morgan's face cleared, and she grinned at Marina, showing off her perfect straight white teeth. "I guess I did hear Liz say you're always late." She laughed.

Marina could feel her cheeks warm, but she kept her smile. It was a constant running joke on the team, and Morgan was part of the team now—there was no reason to be more embarrassed than she normally would be. "Guilty as charged," Marina admitted with a shrug. "But that means I haven't gotten in any practice yet. So, I'd be happy to work with you."

"Thank you," Morgan said.

"No problem," Marina skipped toward the pitcher's mound. "I'm not really a pitcher, you know, but I'll see what I can do." Marina waited until Morgan had squared up and raised her bat, then she started with slow, cautious pitch straight over home plate. Morgan's bat made contact, and Marina jumped into its path, catching the speeding ball.

"Nice catch. So I take it shortstops need to be fast?" Morgan asked.

Marina nodded. "Yup, fastest on the team," she said as she set up to throw again.

"Is that so?" Morgan swung again, and again made contact—this time sending the ball high in the air.

"Yup." Marina shuffled backward until she was under the ball; she let it fall into her glove. She pursed her lips and gave Morgan a teasing smile. "Why? Do you wanna race me or something?" she asked.

Morgan grinned back. "Maybe I do. I'm known for being pretty fast myself."

"So I've heard." Marina once again took a pitcher's stance, and Morgan lifted her bat.

"Yeah?"

"Yeah, and despite other things I've heard, I think maybe I should be giving you more difficult pitches." Marina raised her head and squared her shoulders. Morgan laughed as she tightened her grip on the bat, looking intent on hitting this next pitch. Marina threw, Morgan swung hard and made contact hitting another line-drive, this time straight at Marina, who caught it with a little yelp.

"Are you okay?" Morgan dropped her bat.

"Yeah, just a little surprised is all," Marina laughed. "I thought you were supposed to suck at hitting."

Morgan raised an eyebrow. "Who said that?"

Marina laughed. "You! You've been beating yourself up all afternoon. We can all hear you muttering to yourself, you know."

"Yeah, as a self-coach, I'm a pretty big bitch. But I'm not wrong." Morgan picked up her glove. "Can we throw the ball around for a bit? I want to practice throwing from the base," she said, hitching her thumb toward first.

"Sure," Marina agreed. "Are you at least having fun?"

Morgan nodded. "Yeah, but I'll enjoy it more once I find my feet."

"You seemed to have feet to me," Marina replied in a lighthearted tone as they began to throw the ball back and forth. More than feet, Morgan had *legs*. She had the type of tall, strong build that Marina had always been intensely jealous of. She couldn't help marveling at Morgan's body—it was so perfect—lithe and sculpted. Her look was entirely at odds with the hesitation and uncertainty in her throws and catches. Morgan practiced throwing from first base as Marina moved between the other bases every few throws. Morgan wasn't particularly accurate. Marina had to step off the base to catch the ball most times.

"So, you said before hockey is your sport?" Marina asked.

"Well, it certainly isn't softball." Morgan winced as she caught the ball awkwardly in front of her. She tossed it back. "Yeah, I've been playing hockey since I was a kid."

"That's cool," Marina caught the ball easily. Morgan's aim actually seemed better when she was talking—when she wasn't so hyper-focused on her throws. "Do you play around here?" she asked conversationally.

As Marina coaxed her on, Morgan explained the ins and outs of her hockey league and team. The distraction of the conversation vastly improved Morgan's throws; Marina didn't have to move around so much to catch them. And although Marina didn't follow all the details, the passion with which Morgan spoke was striking. There was so much pride in her voice when she talked about hockey. *She really loves it.* That was obvious. Marina remembered when she used to feel that way about softball. Although she played every year, Marina knew she no longer put the energy into the game she once had. *Maybe helping Morgan get into softball will reignite my own drive.*

"What do you do outside of hockey?" Marina asked when talk of hockey had petered out.

"I'm a dermatologist," Morgan replied.

"Yeah? What's that like?" Marina asked. *A dermatologist is skincare, right? Does that mean she notices all the flaws in my skin when she's looking at me?* Morgan had been looking at her so intently the other day. Marina's skin wasn't perfect—unlike Morgan's, which seemed almost impossibly smooth and even. Paired with her strong, symmetrical features and statuesque body, Morgan could easily have been a model. But instead, she was a doctor, which meant she was smart.

"I like the work I do, and I have a great reputation, so I was recently able to open my own private practice." Morgan grinned. "My patient list is already maxed out."

"Wow, that's… impressive," Marina replied. Something about Morgan's confident pride in work and hockey that was both attractive and off-putting at once. Part of Marina was glad Morgan wasn't very good at softball. *If I'd met her in another context, she would have been hella intimidating. Would I have even talked to her?* Marina wasn't sure she would have, but she was glad that she had. Morgan was curiously compelling.

Chapter 5
Morgan

Morgan had been busy all week with work and home-improvement projects. She was updating her house's main floor bathroom; the process was tedious and time-consuming. When game-day arrived, Morgan was more than ready for a break from renovations. She hadn't gotten to practice since the day of the canceled game. So, she convinced Kelly to meet her at the park early to have a proper warm-up—something that most of the Dirt Bunnies didn't seem to be interested in.

When everybody had arrived, and warm-ups were declared over, Morgan and Kelly retreated to the dugout. As the game got underway, Morgan noticed something she hadn't seen at the previous game.

"Looks like we've got a couple 'fans' today," she said, nodding toward the stands. Two people were loitering on the metal bleachers; judging by the distance between them, they weren't together. One was a thin, attractive woman with long brown hair. She sat on the bottom row, leaning back as if sunning herself. The other was a scruffy-looking guy with greasy, disheveled hair and a bored expression. He was standing in the far corner of the stands—just about as far from the dugout as one could get.

Kelly looked up. "Oh, that's Cassie, Jessica's girlfriend," she said, pointing to the woman. "And over there, I forget his name, but that's Marina's boyfriend."

"Wait, her what?" Morgan was completely thrown for a loop. She would have put good money on Marina being gay. The way she had talked to her and *looked* at her had screamed "lesbian" to Morgan. *Was that all just wishful thinking?*

Morgan looked the man over. Something about him just didn't sit right with her. He and Marina didn't *match*. He looked wimpy. He was short for a man—barely was taller than Marina. Morgan had a good three inches on him. He didn't look particularly athletic either. Morgan made her way toward where the bats lay propped against the wire fence.

"Is that really your boyfriend?" Morgan asked Marina as Marina picked up a bat.

"Yeah, that's Jason. Why?" Marina asked as she gave the bat a few practice swings.

Morgan shrugged and picked up her own bat. "No reason. Just getting the lay of the land." She pushed down any feelings of surprise or disappointment and smiled at Marina. "So, what's the deal with this team we're playing? The Tigers? Not a very original name. Are they any good?" She swung the bat. It was no hockey stick, but Morgan could feel the strength in her arms and the confidence that came with such strength.

"They're alright," Marina said. "They have one chick who strikes out every damn time, but she can catch just about anything, so on balance…" Marina smiled wickedly. "Plus, she's easy on the eyes, if you know what I mean."

Okay, what the hell was that? Morgan wondered. *Was that for my sake because she's aware that I'm gay? Or was I right all along, and this Jason dude is just a slimy little beard?* A beard that looked like he didn't quite understand how to grow a proper beard. Morgan tried to put him out of her mind. She looked at the opposing team. "Which one is she?"

"Blonde ponytail, Twins cap, two o'clock."

Morgan spotted the woman. She was pretty. *She looks a little like me.* That made Morgan smile. *If*

Marina does like women, it seems I might fit her type. Another player caught her eye.

"Oh, hey, I think I recognize that one," she said, pointing. "I'm pretty sure she's one of the goalies I play against at hockey." *A good number of hockey players play softball; I suppose I might run into a few familiar faces.*

"Is she a good goalie?" Marina asked.

"So-so," Morgan said, tilting her hand back and forth. "Her team isn't all that great. My team has only ever lost to them when I wasn't at the game." She grinned at Marina. "But maybe that says more about me than them."

Marina laughed and shook her head. "You are really something, Morgan VanDolen."

"Why's that?" Morgan raised an eyebrow at Marina, whose eyes were bright with amusement. She looked adorable, but Morgan wasn't sure she wanted Marina's mirth to come at her expense.

"You're just so *different* when you talk about hockey compared to when you talk about softball. You're almost like two different people," Marina said.

"Yeah? Which one do you like better?" Morgan asked. "Doctor Hockey and Miss Softball?"

"Why do I feel like it should go the other way around?" Marina tapped her chin.

"I think 'miss' and 'softball' seem to go together for me," Morgan said with a soft chuckle. "And you didn't answer the question."

"I'm just getting to know you both," Marina said. She looked at her. "But I think I could *really* like the Morgan in-between."

Morgan's heart skipped a beat. *How is this not flirting?* Marina was looking up at her with a coy little smile on her delicate lips.

"Well," Morgan said, taking a breath. "I guess I know the Morgan I want to be then."

There was a moment, a pause, the briefest time when they just looked at each other. *What is this?* Morgan wondered. *What is she thinking?* There was a connection between them. Although they barely knew each other, there was something there. *If it isn't a romantic connection, what is it?* Morgan didn't know. But she wanted more than anything to find out.

"Okay, ladies! Let's get this show on the road," Liz's voice cut through, breaking the sweet tension between Morgan and Marina. "Marina, you're up; Rebecca, you're on deck."

Morgan's focus was snapped back to the game and the players around them. With one more little smile, Marina turned and trotted towards the batter's box, ponytail bouncing as she went. *Why does she have to be so cute?* Morgan looked again into the stands at the scrawny boyfriend. *I probably shouldn't hate him just for existing.* But she did. Morgan wrinkled her nose. *Yuck.* She looked back to where Marina was squaring up to the plate. *Yumm.*

Morgan shook her head. *Taken,* she reminded herself. *Focus on her personality, not her looks, VanDolen.* If Morgan couldn't date Marina, she at least wanted the chance to be her friend. *And maybe also my coach.* Morgan pulled on the pair of new batting gloves—an item Marina had encouraged her to buy. Morgan had purchased a bright pink pair last week, and although she'd taken a few practice swings, this was her first chance to wear them in a game.

"So, your whole pink gear obsession is going to carry on past hockey, I see?" Kelly teased as she walked up to stand beside Morgan.

Morgan knew that nobody understood why she wore pink when she played hockey; she didn't like to talk about the reasons behind it. It was personal. And she knew it made her the butt of jokes on her team and a target on the ice. But it was important to her, even if she didn't like explaining why.

"For luck," Morgan said with a nonchalant shrug. "If it works for me there, why not here?"

"Other than the fact that pink is ugly and totally doesn't suit you?" Kelly replied.

"The fact that it doesn't 'suit' me is part of what makes it great." Morgan grinned at her. "I like messing with people."

Morgan thought about Marina's comment about her being two people. Morgan knew there was more to her than most people knew. But it took being vulnerable to allow others in enough to see that. *I am the 'Morgan in-between.'* For some reason, she felt that in time, Marina might be able to see who she really was—the person beyond the accomplishments and bravado.

Morgan's competitive nature overtook her contemplative mood once the game was underway. Any thoughts of 'the Morgan in-between' disappeared the first time she struck out—replaced by focus, determination, and ultimately frustration.

Inning after inning, the Dirt Bunnies failed to score. And after each failed attempt at bat, Morgan grew more agitated and tense. When Dirt Bunnies took the field—and Morgan took her place at first base—she told herself she wouldn't make any more mistakes. But she couldn't seem to make it through a single inning without a reason to be disappointed in herself. She burned with the desire to succeed. She wanted to be part of the solution, not the problem. But the harder she pushed herself, the worse she seemed to perform.

"Morgan, if you can, try and throw the ball instead of running," Liz coached in the fifth inning as they transitioned to fielding. "You are a very fast runner, but a thrown ball is faster." Liz's voice was sweet and positive and a little condescending.

"Yeah, I know. I'm sorry." Morgan clenched her jaw against her embarrassment. It was the same damn principle as in hockey—a pass is faster than skating the puck. *Obviously*. This was just a ball instead of a puck; it should be second nature.

"It's okay, don't worry. It's only your second game, and overall you're doing great," Liz said, patting Morgan on the back. Morgan clenched her jaw tighter; it was mortifying. She wanted to say that, of course, she knew throwing the ball would be faster than *running* it in from the outfield. But her mistakes had cost the team two runs—mistakes she would not have made if she'd been confident in the accuracy of her throws.

The next inning, Morgan tried to make up for her past mistakes but over-corrected—throwing the ball too quickly before she'd properly established *where* to throw it.

"That was better!" Liz chirped when their time in the field ended. "Just remember, stopping a run is more important than just getting an out, okay?"

"Yeah, I know. Sorry." Morgan's jaw was starting to hurt from clenching. She walked—taking slow, measured steps—back to her place on the bench and sat down. She didn't look at her teammates but kept her gaze fixed on the ground. *Take a deep breath, VanDolen*, she coached herself. *And chill the fuck out.*

"Liz means well, you know," a soft familiar voice said.

"Huh?" Morgan looked up. Marina stood before her, her dark eyes trained on Morgan's face.

"Liz," Marina clarified. "She means well when she coaches, but she can also be kind of hard to take sometimes. Peppy criticism just doesn't always sit right, you know?" Marina was looking at her with that Mona Lisa smile again.

She's perceptive. Morgan wondered if Marina had noticed the disappointment she'd felt when Marina had pointed out her boyfriend earlier. *How clearly do I display my emotions?* Morgan obviously wasn't particularly good at hiding her frustration.

"It's okay. I appreciate a little constructive criticism," Morgan insisted. "It's honestly better than everybody telling me I'm doing 'great' all the time when it's painfully obvious that I'm not."

"Well, in that case…" Marina's smile grew ever so slightly, a twinkle in her eye. "Relax, for fuck's sake. The more you beat yourself up, the worse you play. Next time you're up to bat, just have fun with it. You said you know that player on the other team, right?"

"Yeah, so?"

"So, talk to her. She's the catcher; strike up a conversation when you're up," Marina suggested.

"But shouldn't I be focused?"

Marina shook her head. "When we were practicing the other day—I don't know if you realized it, but you did much better when we were chatting than when you were 'focused.' Maybe you can recreate that if you chat with her a little."

Morgan considered Marina's idea. She didn't honestly see how 'chatting' with some vague acquaintance would help anything. But she nodded. "Okay, I'll give it a shot."

Morgan pulled on her batting gloves and stepped up to the plate. She looked at the pitcher, squatting behind home plate. Her catcher's mask was reminiscent of a hockey cage, and it made Morgan even more certain that she was who Morgan thought she was.

"Hey, you play hockey, don't you?" Morgan asked conversationally.

The woman looked up. "Yeah, I—" The woman stopped, her eyes flicking to Morgan's pink batting gloves, recognition spreading over her face. It was not a friendly expression. "You're the one who wears all that pink… stuff."

"Yeah, that's me." Morgan smiled thinly and lifted the bat. The first pitch was a little outside, and Morgan didn't swing.

"Ball one," the ump called.

"You're a goalie, right?" Morgan asked.

The catcher tossed the ball back to her pitcher. "Yup," she said simply, indicating with that single syllable that she wasn't a big fan of Morgan or this conversation.

"I thought so." Morgan smirked. "I remember scoring on you."

The pitch came before the goalie-catcher had time to reply. Morgan swung. She made contact, and the ball flew into the outfield and landed on the grass between outfielders. Morgan dropped the bat and ran. She kept an eye on the field where the other team was scrambling for the ball as she rounded first and made for second. The outfielder scooped up the ball and threw it, but Morgan beat the throw. She took a few deep breaths; she'd never hit a double before. Her team cheered for her, and she grinned back at them. Marina caught her eye and gave her two thumbs up. Morgan felt her grin widen.

At home plate, Kelly stepped up to bat. Behind her, the catcher was glaring at Morgan. *If she disliked me before, she probably hates me now. It's a good thing softball isn't much of a contact sport.* Morgan chuckled to herself. *Or else she might hit me.*

Kelly was picky about her pitches and was rewarded by being walked to first. Morgan waited for Liz to step up to the plate. Morgan was tense—her whole body tingled with nervous excitement. She wanted to make it to third. She yearned to score a run—if she did, it would be her first. *Half-way there. Come on, Liz, bring me home.*

Liz hit a grounder, and Morgan sprinted for third. But the shortstop scooped up the ball and tossed it to third, easily beating her there. "Out."

"Fuck," Morgan swore as she walked dejectedly off the field.

Marina met her there, smiling. "Nice work! See, I told you a little friendly conversation would relax you."

Morgan snorted. "The conversation wasn't particularly friendly. I don't think that chick likes me very much. Not that many of my opponents do."

"Oh." Marina's smile faded.

"But it still did the trick," Morgan added quickly, grinning at Marina. "Thanks, coach." She winked, and Marina's smile returned, her cheeks going pink.

Morgan's was the second out of the inning. The team earned two runs before Jessica struck out and sent the Dirt Bunnies back out into the field. Morgan took her place at first in better spirits than she had been in all game. Whether or not Marina's advice had been the reason, Morgan was happy with her double *and* with the attention she was getting from Marina. The whole team was giddy with optimism; the last two runs had tied up the game, giving them a chance at winning.

When the goalie-catcher was up to bat, Morgan crossed her fingers. "Please strike out," she mumbled under her breath. No such luck. The woman hit the ball; it bounced off the grass and into Rebecca's glove. She quickly threw it to Morgan, but Morgan fumbled the catch, and the ball hit the dirt. While she scrambled to pick it up, the goalie-catcher arrived safely on base.

"Son of a bitch," Morgan swore under her breath as she tossed the ball to Kelly.

The woman smirked at her. "You may think you're God's gift to hockey, but you're on my field now," she said acerbically. It took all Morgan had to turn away and not punch the woman in her smug face. Morgan's chest burning with renewed anger and embarrassment—the pride she'd felt at her earlier accomplishment too quickly overshadowed by her latest failure.

The game ended in a heartbreaking narrow loss for the Dirt Bunnies. Morgan's frustration already made her tense and unhappy; when the game ended and Marina trotted over to her boyfriend, Morgan's mood darkened further. She watched with bitter jealousy as Marina's boyfriend put his arm around Marina's shoulders and kissed her. Seeing them together was like pouring rubbing alcohol on a fresh wound. It stung like hell.

Let it go, VanDolen. There's nothing you can do about that, but there is something you can do about your shitty softball skills.

Morgan didn't even bother staying for post-game beers. She went back to her house to work on her renovations and make plans to improve her game. By the end of the night, she'd made significant progress on the house and had ordered some softball training equipment. It was expensive, but it if could help, it was worth it. There were ten more games left in the season. And before those ten games were over, Morgan would be a true softball player. And if she had her way, Marina would be a true friend.

Chapter 6
Marina

As she did every day, Marina arrived home and immediately went to her bedroom to change out of her "business attire." She managed a bank, which required her to dress formally, and it was her least favorite part of the job. She was mathematically inclined and good with people, plus she loved the quiet environment of her small branch. But the uniform of dress pants, heels, button-up, and blazer was like a straight-jacket. It made her feel confined and uncomfortable all day. Coming home and trading it in for soft, comfy clothes was the best part of her day.

Marina pulled off her pants, unbuttoned her shirt, and tossed both in the hamper. "Ahhh," she sighed audibly as she unhooked her bra and let the underwire torture device slip off her shoulders to fall on the floor. She stood for a moment in nothing but her underwear, cupping her small breasts and relishing the freedom of near-nudity. It had been a long day—not a bad day, but tiring, nonetheless.

Jason's dog, a beagle-lab mix named Scout, scampered into the room and hopped up on her bed.

"Hey, buddy," Marina said to him, dropping her hands from her chest. "Want to go for a walk?"

Scout jumped back off the bed, his tail wagging so hard the whole back half of him wagged with it. Marina pulled on a sports bra, black yoga pants, and a Twins t-shirt. She walked out of the bedroom, across the small house to the living room, where Jason was sitting playing video games—seemingly oblivious to her presence.

"Hey," Marina said.

"Hey," Jason parroted, his eyes ever leaving the screen.

"How was your day?" she asked.

"Meh." Jason shrugged.

"I'm going to walk the dog," she said. "Want to come with?"

"Naw." Jason was mono-syllabic at the moment, apparently. Marina rolled her eyes. *Boys.* She passed through the living room to the kitchen, where Scout's leash hung on a hook. She clipped it to his collar, slipped on her sneakers, and stepped out the side door into the warm evening air.

"Which way today?" Marina asked her dog. "How about toward the ballpark?" Scout tugged at his leash in the direction of the park. She was sure he hadn't actually understood her, but she was glad he seemed to agree. She liked the loop she and Scout often took through the neighborhood and around the two baseball diamonds in the center of the small city park. They started off in that direction. The sun was still high in the summer evening sky, but the temperature was mild. It was a perfect night for a walk. Marina's eyes wandered across her neighbors' front yards as she walked. There was a comfortable familiarity to her neighborhood that Marina loved—the sidewalks, modest houses, and old-growth trees gave the area a classic "Everytown America" feeling. And although Marina wasn't acquainted with all of her neighbors, there was a sense of community about the place.

Marina and Scout turned the corner, bringing the ballpark into view. The park looked empty. Neither diamond was occupied, and the concession stands were closed. But from the other side of the concession building, Marina heard the clink of a bat hitting a ball.

Somebody must be using the batting cages. She and Scout rounded the corner of the building into view of the batting cages. Marina caught sight of a familiar blonde braid.

"Morgan?" Marina blinked. She hadn't expected to run into Morgan randomly like this. She looked around, but Morgan seemed to be alone.

Morgan turned, and her face lit up; her bright blue eyes seemed to sparkle in the sunlight. "Oh, hey, Marina!" she said. "What are you doing here?"

"Just taking the dog for a walk," Marina answered, even though it seemed self-evident; Scout was tugging at his leash and whining impatiently. He didn't like to stop during walks except to sniff interesting things. Apparently, the edge of the batting cages didn't catch his olfactory interest.

"Do you live around here?" Morgan asked.

"Yeah, I'm a couple blocks that way," Marina said, hitching her thumb west, in the direction of home. "You?"

"About half a mile up," Morgan replied, pointing to the northeast—practically the opposite direction.

"I didn't know you lived so close," Marina said. "I was under the impression that you weren't from around here." When Morgan had told her that she was a dermatologist with a new house, Marina had pictured something big and shiny—not the type of thing you'd find around here.

Morgan shrugged. "I'm new. I just moved in this past spring, and I basically spend all my time either at work, hockey, or fixing up the house. I haven't really explored the neighborhood much yet."

"Well, welcome. It's a great town, I really…" Marina trailed off. She'd noticed something over Morgan's shoulder that she'd never seen in one of the batting cages at the park before: a pitching machine. "Where'd that come from?" she asked, looking curiously at the contraption—spinning white wheel and spiral hopper that stood on three blue legs.

"It's mine," Morgan said with another nonchalant shrug. The wheel was still spinning, but the hopper was empty; Morgan reached back and switched it off.

Marina looked quizzically at her. "When did you…? Aren't you new to softball?"

"Yeah, that's why I needed it," Morgan said with a chuckle. "After that last game, I realized that I would need to get serious about training if I want to stop embarrassing myself."

"You're not embarrassing yourself." Marina rolled her eyes.

"I just want to feel more confident." Morgan dropped her bat and began retrieving balls from around the cage. "It's too bad that it doesn't help me with throwing and catching."

"Your catching is fine," Marina insisted.

"Don't you remember when I dropped the ball and let that lady from hockey onto first?" Morgan asked.

Marina shook her head. "Nobody but you would remember a little thing like that, Morgan."

"Well, I remember. She was kind of a dick about it, actually." Morgan folded her arms and frowned, her blonde brows furrowed. "Beside which, anybody with eyes will have notices that my throwing is atrocious. Especially over long distances." She gave Marina a look that dared her to disagree.

Marina didn't argue the point. In truth, Morgan didn't have the best arm. "If you ever want to practice throwing some time, apparently we're practically neighbors, so…" Marina trailed off with a vague gesture.

"You'd help me practice?" Morgan asked, eyebrows raised. "I mean more than you already did at the practice the other day?"

"I'd throw the ball around with you. Don't make it sound so serious," Marina teased.

"Are you up for 'throwing the ball around' a bit tonight?" Morgan asked eagerly, catching Marina off-guard.

"Oh, well, uh," she looked down at Scout. "I'd have to bring the dog home and check—" She was about to say, "check with Jason," but for some reason, she stopped herself. "Uh, to get my glove."

"That's okay, I can wait. I'll hit a few more here," Morgan said, indicating the machine.

"Okay, sure. I guess I'll see you in a few minutes." Marina turned and walked the two and a half blocks back to her little unassuming stucco house. She went back in through the side door to the kitchen.

"I'm back," she called out to Jason as she stepped inside, through the kitchen, and into the living room. Jason was still sitting on the sofa playing his game—exactly as she had left him. "I'm heading back out again, though," she added.

"What?" Jason asked blandly.

"I ran into somebody from my softball team; we're going to play a little catch, I guess," she said. Jason didn't respond. "Is that cool with you?" Marina asked.

"Sure," Jason said, his eyes still glued to the screen. Mild annoyance rippled through Marina. *Would it kill him to use more than one word at a time?*

"Okay, well, uh. Bye again," Marina said. She picked up her mitt on the way out and trotted down the street to the ballpark, where Morgan was still hitting ball after ball. Marina watched her. Morgan had a death grip on the bat and was swinging at every ball like she was trying to bust the seams open. She clearly had power, but she could benefit from a little finesse.

The pitching machine ran out of balls, and Morgan turned to look at Marina. "Any tips before I call it a day on batting practice?" The look in her eyes was so intense.

"Well... I've already told you to relax... Maybe work on your form?" Marina advised cautiously, not sure how Morgan would take a new line of critique.

"What about my form?" Morgan asked, sounding genuinely interested and not at all defensive.

"I don't know that I could pinpoint something specific. I'm not really a coach," Marina said with an apologetic shrug. "I just know what looks right and what feels right. I'm not confident that I can explain it well. Maybe look for videos online?"

"Yeah, I've watched a couple." Morgan sighed, dropped her bat, and began taking off her pink batting gloves. "Maybe I should try taking a video of myself to compare side-by-side," she mused.

"You're really into this improvement thing," Marina said as Morgan began to pack up her gear, including the pitching machine.

"I just don't see the point in half-assing something. If I'm going to take the time to do it, I'm going to full-ass it."

Marina giggled. "Full-assing, huh?"

"Yup," Morgan grinned. "Us hockey chicks are renowned for our full asses, you know," she said, slapping her backside.

"I did not know that," Marina said with another giggle. She wasn't about to admit it, but she *had* noticed Morgan's fantastic ass.

Morgan grunted as she picked up the pitching machine. "Learn something new every day," she huffed as she waddled out of the batting cage, awkwardly carrying the heavy device with her bag slung across her back.

"Can I help you with that somehow?" Marina offered.

Morgan shook her head. "I think I've got it. My jeep's just right over there." She nodded toward the parking lot. Marina watched her, feeling a little guilty for not offering to help sooner. *I could have at least carried her bag for her.*

Morgan shook out her arms once the machine was safely tucked into the trunk. "Oof, I am going to be sore tomorrow."

"Are you still up for throwing the ball around for a bit?" Marina asked. It had been Morgan's idea, and yet somehow Marina suddenly felt awkward—as if she were asking for a favor.

"Oh, absolutely!" Morgan pulled out her glove and a ball. "Want to head out onto the field or—"

Morgan was interrupted by the sound of a large pickup truck thumping with music. It pulled into the lot, followed behind by one car after another. Young men in matching baseball caps began to pile out of the vehicles.

"It looks like somebody else has the field now," Marina said, stating the obvious.

"Want to head over to my yard instead? I've got beer too if that interests you," Morgan offered.

"Sure, sounds great," Marina agreed without a second thought. The two jumped into Morgan's jeep and rolled out, putting the field in the rearview mirror.

"It's not far," Morgan called over the wind of driving in an open-top jeep.

"Yeah, you mentioned," Marina called back.

"I only drove because I brought the pitching machine," Morgan added.

"I figured," Marina said. "Oh, is this your house?" she asked as Morgan pulled into the driveway that ran beside a small cottage-style house with white siding, dark green trim, and a cute little front porch.

"Sure is," Morgan confirmed. "The outside still needs some work."

"Really? I think it's adorable as it is!" Marina assured her.

"Thanks." Morgan parked just outside the detached garage and hopped out. Marina followed her to the backyard. It was a large yard for the area—flat with lush green grass and one small maple tree on the far side. There was a tiny deck on the back of the house with barely enough space for a grill, table, and two chairs.

"I'm going to rip out that deck and put in a new one," Morgan said, following Marina's gaze. "It's on my list for this summer."

"Yeah, wood decks are a pain like that. I'm glad we have a patio instead."

"We?" Morgan echoed. "You and your boyfriend have a house together?"

"Sorta," Marina shrugged. "It's my house, but he lives there too." She didn't know what she had to feel embarrassed about. Nonetheless, she could feel her cheeks burning, and she knew she was blushing. Jason had moved in over a year ago. He and had yet to pay a cent toward rent or utilities, despite treating the place as if it were his own. Marina often felt ashamed of herself for not addressing the situation with him. But Morgan wasn't aware of any of that.

"So, building your own porch, huh?" Marina said, redirecting away from anything Jason-related. "You must be handy."

"It's a lesbian stereotype for a reason, you know." She winked, and Marina felt her cheeks pink again.

"You're a lesbian?" Marina asked.

"Yup," Morgan nodded. "And honestly I thought you were too when we first met. Before I saw your boyfriend at the—."

"I'm bi," Marina said, the words coming out fast and short, like an unexpected sneeze.

"Ohhh!" Morgan exclaimed, chuckling. "That makes more sense."

Marina didn't quite comprehend what Morgan meant by that, but she was already feeling too flustered and embarrassed to ask. "Come on," she said, punching her fist into her glove. "Are we going to 'practice' or what, VanDolen?"

Morgan grinned and tossed her the ball.

"So, what do you do for work?" Morgan inquired as they threw the ball back and forth.

"I manage the local bank; it's a block off Main Street," Marina answered.

"Do you like it?" Morgan asked, sounding skeptical.

"Yeah, it's alright." Marina shrugged. "You said before you're a dermatologist, right?"

"Yup," Morgan confirmed.

"So, is being a dermatologist anything like that show, Dr. Pimple Popper?" Marina asked, mainly as a joke.

Morgan groaned loudly. "Ugh, I *detest* that show. Everybody always has to ask about it these days."

"Sorry," Marina said.

"Don't be." Morgan took a few steps back and would up to throw the ball again. "Hey, would you mind if I did it fast and hard?"

"That's what she said!" Marina blurted out without thinking. She smacked her forehead. "Sorry, dumb habit I picked up from my boyfriend."

Morgan chuckled. "I don't mind one bit. I can appreciate a good dirty joke."

Marina helped Morgan with her harder throws for the rest of the evening. Morgan was even less accurate when throwing hard; she gave Marina quite a workout. But it was fun—chatting and throwing, with a little bit of good-natured taunting and a lot of laughter. The time flew by. Marina didn't even realize how long it had been until she noticed that it was so dark she could hardly see the ball anymore.

"I think we need to call it a night," Marina said. "It's the sun's almost totally down."

"Oh, wow." Morgan looked around. "You know I didn't even notice."

"Yeah, me neither, until just now," Marina said. She chuckled. "Any darker, and things could have gotten dangerous."

"Dangerous?" Morgan repeated.

"Your aim is iffy as it is; I worry that in the dark, you'd bean me in the head or something," Marina teased.

"If I got you in the head, I think that would mean my aim was pretty good," Morgan countered with a laugh.

"Touché," Marina conceded. She smiled at Morgan. "This was fun."

"It really was," Morgan agreed. "We should do it again sometime."

"Yeah, for sure."

The dim evening light on Morgan's face made her look like she'd stepped out of an old French painting. *She is incredibly beautiful, isn't she?* She was just the kind of woman Marina might have been interested in if she weren't dating Jason. *There's no way I'd have the confidence to ask somebody like her out. She's out of my league. What lesbian wants to date an inexperienced bi chick anyway? Nobody, that's who.*

"What?" Morgan asked, and Marina realized she'd been staring.

She shook her head and began to back away toward the driveway. "Nothing, sorry. Zoned out. I must be tired. I should get going home."

"Want to come in for a beer first? I can show you around the house," Morgan offered, but Marina shook her head again.

"Sorry. Another time. I'm sure Jason is wondering where I am," she lied. She doubted very much that Jason even realized she wasn't home. But her earlier train of thought had made her hyper-aware of just how attracted to Morgan she was, and she wasn't sure how she felt about that.

"Well, can I give you a ride then?" Morgan suggested.

"Oh, no, that's okay. It's less than a mile. I can walk," Marina replied.

"Are you sure?" Morgan pressed.

"Positive. I like walking." Marina thought she saw disappointment in Morgan's expression, but it was hard to read her face in the dim light. "But let's for sure do this again soon," Marina added. "Next time, we can plan in advance to set aside time for that beer and house tour. I'd love to see all the work you've done."

"Alright, sounds good." Morgan waved. "See ya later then, Marina."

"Yeah, bye, Morgan," Marina said before turning and walking away.

Chapter 7
Morgan

As Morgan watched Marina walk away, a warm sensation filled her chest, like the embers of a dying fire. The feeling was at once happy and sorrowful. *Marina is bi. But she's taken.* Being aware that Marina did like women would make getting over her crush just that much harder. The fact that she had a chance, however slim, would sustain that flame. Even if Morgan didn't want it to.

There's nothing to be done, so let it go. Marina was obviously in a long-term serious relationship. Morgan was no longer the type of person who would try to break anybody up; she'd gone down that path before. Her natural instinct had always been to go after what she wanted—it still was, for the most part. But she had learned the hard way that "getting the girl" doesn't often work out unless the girl was free to be "gotten" in the first place. *That doesn't mean I can't try to get closer to her as a friend.*

Morgan turned, stepped up onto the deck, and walked into her house through the sliding glass door that led to her dining area. Morgan picked up her phone and texted Marina, "I had fun today. Let's plan a time when we can hang out for longer and I can give you a tour of the house. We can make it a kind of pizza-and-practice thing."

"Absolutely!" Marina texted back right away. "I probably can't do it until after the next game tho."

"That's fine!" They exchanged a few more texts until they had a day and time set for their "pizza-and-practice" get-together.

Morgan looked around her house. She still had projects she would like to put the finishing touches on before she gave Marina the tour, but all her big projects on the main floor were complete. The last time the house had any renovations done was in the 1970s, but most of it had barely been touched since it was built back in the 50s. The main floor had been chopped up into four separate rooms—living room, kitchen, dining room, and a small bedroom—plus the bathroom.

With some help from a contractor and a lot of her own labor, Morgan had taken down the walls between the kitchen, living room, and dining room and created one large open space. She'd laid hardwood floors end to end, making it all feel cohesive. She'd extended the kitchen into what had been the dining room, adding new white cabinets and dark quartz countertops. She didn't need a formal dining room, just enough space for a small four-top table that sat at the back so that she could look through the large sliding glass doors out to the back yard when she ate. Morgan loved her living space. Everything was new and just how she liked it: clean and simple.

She'd turned the main floor bedroom into a home office with a pull-out sofa for the rare instances when she had overnight company. She didn't use the room often. Aside from new floors and a coat of paint, there hadn't been much to do there. The bathroom was the final project on the first floor. Dated, grimy, and pink, Morgan had torn the whole thing out. Her penchant for pink didn't extend past her sports gear and certainly wouldn't stand in a bathroom.

That project had been the most frustrating. She wasn't a fan of plumbing work. Nothing ever seemed to go right the first time around. But the real killer was the floors and shower. The tile pattern she'd fallen in love with proved to be a massive pain in the ass to lay to her exacting standards. But all the sweat and consternation she put into it made it her proudest achievement in the house.

Morgan made herself dinner, ate, and did the dishes while listening to her latest audiobook. She loved listening to books. Audiobooks had been her closest companions during her renovations. Living alone could be lonely sometimes, but Morgan didn't mind when she had a good book.

She continued to listen to her book as she finished putting up the new light fixture over her kitchen table. By the time she'd finished, it was late. *Oops, it's past my bedtime.* She tidied up from her project, locked the doors, shut off the lights, and headed up the stairs.

The master suite took up the entire top floor. Morgan hadn't renovated it yet, but she had big plans. As it stood, the room screamed 'cheap seventies addition' with its busy wallpaper and orange shag carpet that extended into the bathroom. Morgan changed for bed and brushed her teeth, looking at her reflection in the cracked old mirror. She was itching to start tearing the tiny bathroom apart.

Morgan climbed into bed thinking about the house, but when she closed her eyes, her thoughts wandered from floorplans to softball diamonds and from there to Marina. Morgan could see Marina in her mind's eye—beautiful, mysterious Marina. Morgan had learned a few new things about Marina today: Marina had a dog, worked at a bank, and lived with her boyfriend. Morgan tried not to think about that last part. *Marina didn't tell me much about her job; we went right back to talking about mine.* Morgan worried that she'd spent too much time talking about herself. Marina had encouraged her with lots of follow-up questions about everything she'd said, but that didn't mean she really wanted to Morgan go on and on all the time. *I should make more effort to ask her about herself next time.*

Fortunately, Morgan saw Marina shortly thereafter. Unfortunately, when she did see her, they barely had a moment to speak, much less hold a real conversation. Marina was late, as usual. And she brought her boyfriend with her, who seemed chattier and more engaged with the game than last time. Between those factors and Morgan's concentration on her own playing, the only interaction she and Marina had—aside from on the field—was to confirm their upcoming "pizza and practice" session.

Part of Morgan had wished that it could be a date, but as she'd watched Marina leave the park with Jason, she knew it could never be. *I really do need the practice; focus on that, VanDolen*, she reminded herself. The game was a lackluster win, with Morgan doing absolutely nothing to contribute. The Dirt Bunnies didn't seem to care that Morgan was still basically deadweight. They refused to even acknowledge her failures. In fact, Liz and Kelly had been visibly frustrated by Morgan's self-criticisms and had refused to coach her on how to improve.

"You're fine," was all they had to offer when she'd asked how she could better prioritize where to throw the ball during plays. "Just have fun," they said when she grumbled about causing an out. *How can I get better if nobody will tell me what I'm doing wrong?* It made Morgan wonder if she would have a better softball experience on a different team. *But other teams don't have Marina.* Marina was the only one who seemed willing to actively help.

Marina showed up right on time for their "practice and pizza" not-a-date date. Morgan was waiting for her on the deck when she walked up the driveway. Marina looked as pretty as ever in black leggings and a green, flowy tank top. She often wore similar outfits at softball; only today, she had left her hair down. It came to her shoulders in perfect ringlets that looked so soft Morgan had to fight a sudden urge to touch them.

"You're not late," Morgan exclaimed with a teasing grin. "I'm shocked!"

Marina groaned. "Ugh, not you too. The team makes me sound much worse than I really am—I'll have you know."

"I don't know. I think this is the first time I've ever seen you show up to something on time. That makes you… what, one for five?" Morgan gave Marina what she hoped came across as a playful smile. "Their 'opinion' on the matter seems pretty accurate to me."

"Oh, shut up," Marina said, a small smile curling her lips, her curls bouncing as she shook her head. "Are we going to throw the ball around a little or what?"

"That's the plan," Morgan agreed, picking her glove up from the table, slipping it on, and hopping off the deck.

"Our last game went pretty well, don't you think?" Marina said as they began to throw the ball across the yard.

"I guess," Morgan agreed half-heartedly.

"You guess? We murdered them." Marina gave her a quizzical look.

Morgan shrugged. "I could have played better." The fact that they'd beat the team so easily and Morgan *still* had yet to score a run bothered her.

"You are improving, you know," Marina said, purposefully throwing the ball wide of Morgan so that she would have to move to catch it, which she did… barely.

"See?" Marina pointed out as if that one decent catch was proof.

"Maybe. But I still have a long way to go." Morgan considered imitating Marina's wide toss, but she was still working on her accuracy, so she aimed to throw the ball directly at Marina hard and on target. It was almost on target. Just a little short. "I really appreciate you practicing with me," Morgan added.

"Of course, any time," Marina said, diving forward to catch the ball. She pushed her curls out of her face. "Oof, hold on a second." She dropped her glove and moved to pull her hair into a ponytail. Morgan sighed in disappointment. She liked seeing Marina's hair down. It was so cute when she pushed it out of her eyes.

"What?" Marina looked up at the sound of Morgan's sigh.

"Oh, nothing." Morgan couldn't tell her how attractive her loose curls were; that would be weird. "I just... I don't understand why my desire to get better seems to rub people on the team the wrong way so much," Morgan said. It wasn't what had been on her mind, but it was still true.

"I don't get it either, honestly," Marina said. She'd finished pulling her hair back but hadn't resumed throwing the ball. She walked across the lawn to be closer to Morgan as they talked. "I think what you're doing is brave," she said, smiling at her in that unreadable way.

"What's brave?" Morgan asked, confused.

"I think it's brave to try something new and when it's not a perfect fit right away, to not quit," Marina clarified.

"VanDolens don't quit." Morgan narrowed her eyes at Marina, a thought striking her. "Hey, are you saying I'm so bad that if you were me, you'd quit?"

Marina's cheeks went pink in a cute, freckled blush. "Honestly, yes," she admitted. "But that says more about me than about your playing. I've played softball

all my life. If I ever got up the courage to try something new, I just know I'd give up the second I hit a bump. I like safe and easy."

"Where's the adventure in that?" Morgan asked. It sounded like the exact opposite of her own take on life: find a challenge, conquer it, and then find a new one. That was the VanDolen way.

"Maybe I'm not looking for adventure," Marina said defensively. "Maybe I just want to enjoy the things I know I like. Then I can enjoy them to their fullest without any of that pesky self-doubt or beginner's nerves."

"Doesn't that get boring?" Morgan asked.

Marina shrugged one shoulder. "Maybe that's why I like helping you learn. It's new and interesting but still safely in my wheelhouse."

"So, what you're saying is, this season would be boring without me," Morgan teased, wiggling her eyebrows.

Marina shook her head, the curls of her ponytail bouncing with the motion. "Softball would never be boring to me. But I really am enjoying seeing the sport I love through somebody else's eyes." Marina looked at Morgan—her big brown eyes looking at her as if she were seeing right into Morgan's soul. Morgan searched those eyes—that Mona Lisa expression—looking for any hint as to what Marina was thinking. *What does she see when she looks at me like that?* But Marina's mind was still a puzzle to Morgan; she radiated kindness and warmth, but her thoughts were well hidden away.

"You should try hockey some time," Morgan suggested. "Then maybe I can see in you what you're seeing in me."

Marina laughed; her sweet voice made laughter sound like music. "All you'd see if I tried hockey would be me falling on my ass."

Morgan shook her head adamantly. "I have a hard time believing that. You're so athletic and coordinated. You'd be a natural."

"I bet that's what Kelly thought about you when she brought you onto the team. But look how that turned out," Marina teased.

Morgan laughed, even though the joke had stung just a little bit. "It's not over yet," she said.

"No, but I think this game of catch is." Marina rubbed at her stomach. "I'm starving. Didn't you say something about pizza?"

"I'd like to practice a little more," Morgan said, disappointed.

"I'll make you a deal," Marina said. "We get pizza now, you give me the house tour you've been promising, and after that, we can go down to the ballpark and see if we can get in a little batting practice."

Morgan grinned. "That sounds perfect."

As they looked over the pizza menu together, Morgan and Marina discovered they had very similar tastes. There were several things they could have chosen. In the end, they settled on ordering a large veggie supreme.

Marina rubbed her hands together and hummed happily. "Mmmm. I'm, like, ridiculously excited for this pizza," she said.

"Why this pizza in particular?" Morgan asked, surprised by the giddy excitement emanating off Marina.

"Oh, Jason hates all vegetables. It's pepperoni or meat-lovers, always," Marina explained, rolling her eyes. "If I so much as hint at the idea of something 'vegetarian,' he gags like a twelve-year-old."

"So why not just get your own pizza?"

Marina cocked her head. "Huh. I had honestly never thought of that… It seems like a lot of pizza…" She shrugged. "Maybe I will, or maybe it'll just be another bonus of hanging out with you: good pizza." Marina gave Morgan a sly smile that made Morgan's heart skip a beat.

"That's alright with me," she said, grinning back at Marina.

While they waited for the pizza to arrive, Morgan gave Marina a tour of the main level of the house. Marina was clearly impressed. She whistled as she ran her hands along to cool stone countertops. "It's gorgeous. I wish my kitchen were half as nice. It's all Formica, linoleum, and bad wallpaper. This is like a dream kitchen. The whole house is beautiful, really."

"Thank you. It turned out well," Morgan said, swelling with pride.

Marina's brows furrowed slightly, and she glanced around. "What about the bedroom, though? I haven't seen any bedrooms. I mean, I guess you told me that front office is technically a bedroom, but clearly, you don't sleep there."

Morgan pointed at the ceiling. "My room is upstairs. But I haven't gotten around to renovating—"

"Can I see it?" Marina asked.

Morgan was somewhat taken aback by how boldly such a new acquaintance had asked to see her private space. At the same time, part of her wanted nothing more than to bring Marina up to her bedroom.

"If you're interested, absolutely," Morgan agreed.

"I'm sure the 'after' will be even that much more impressive if I've seen the 'before,'" Marina pointed out as Morgan led her up the stairs.

"Fair point," Morgan agreed. "Just don't judge me for the state it's in now. It really is a disaster."

"I'd never judge. My house is always a disaster," Marina dismissed her. "It's nice that you have this second floor. My attic is unfinished, although you're giving me ideas."

Morgan stood aside at the top of the stairs to give Marina the full view. "See, I told you it's a wreck."

"It's not a wreck," Marina wandered through the room. "I mean that carpet, wow. But it's still so tidy." Marina ran her hand over the duvet. "I like your bed."

"Thank you," Morgan rasped. Watching Marina touch her bed had sent shivers across her skin. Visions of pulling Marina down onto the soft mattress flooded Morgan's mind. She cleared her throat, pushing away such thoughts. "I'm a bit of a 'neat freak.' It comes with the type-A territory."

Marina laughed as she continued her circle around the room. When she stepped into the bathroom, Morgan winced inwardly. No matter how 'tidy' she was or how much she cleaned, it always looked disgusting.

"I don't think I've ever seen carpet in a bathroom before," Marina said with a giggle when she'd reemerged.

"I'm going to rip that up for certain," Morgan said, letting out the breath she'd been holding. *Did I think she was going to run in horror or something?* Morgan wrinkled her nose. "The whole thing is a total gut-job," she said.

"Tell me about your plans," Marina said, and Morgan did, laying out exactly what she had in mind for the whole attic suite. She intended to build a new, larger bathroom and expand the closet to create a walk-in. The projects would take up substantial space from the bedroom. It would be complicated due to the sloped ceilings, but Morgan was confident she could pull it off. There was so much potential in this house. That's why she had bought it. Marina listened intently; she seemed genuinely interested in the process.

"When do you plan to start on that? Maybe I can come help paint or something," Marina offered as the two tramped back down the stairs.

"That could be fun," Morgan said, although she was usually too "type-A" to accept help from non-professionals. "But I'm not going to get to it until the fall. I want to get some outdoor projects—" Morgan was cut off by the ringing of the doorbell. "Oh, pizza's here!"

She and Marina ate together in the kitchen before heading back outside to practice, just as Marina had suggested. It was a nearly perfect evening—only Morgan's unrequited crush on her new friend kept it from being *perfect* perfect. Pizza, sports, and great company—life didn't get a whole lot better than that.

Chapter 8
Marina

Marina and Morgan made "softball and takeout hang-outs" a regular event. They got together so frequently they decided to move beyond pizza, expanding their dinner options by trying different takeout foods from various local restaurants. Tonight, they'd ordered from the Vietnamese place on Main Street. Marina had wanted to try it for ages, but Jason insisted the restaurant "smelled funny" from the sidewalk and therefore couldn't possibly be any good. He was wrong. It was delicious. Both she and Morgan had scarfed the food down like a couple of high school football players. It was fun to have a friend with such an incredibly similar taste in food—even if Morgan's spice tolerance was a bit higher. Marina licked her lips. She could still feel the slight after-burn of the "hot and spicy wings" Morgan had insisted she try. Marina lightly touched her fingers to her mouth. *We'll have to order those again.*

The sun had long since gone down when Marina turned the corner onto her block. The streetlamps and trees worked together to create long shadows that striped the road in light and dark. It had become a habit for she and Morgan to lose track of time—relying on the setting sun to tell them their evening was over. But even in the dark and from several houses away, Marina could see Jason and his friends outside. They were hanging out—either sitting on the side steps or leaning against the house—smoking and chatting under the single floodlight, Scout laying at their feet.

A rumble of laughter erupted from the group, and Marina's smile grew. She liked seeing Jason having fun with Evan and Matt, his two best buddies from high school. Although not long ago, she'd felt differently. She had often been bitter about the time he spent with his friends—time she thought he should have spent with her. She'd felt lonely and abandoned when the three were together, even when she hung around with them.

Marina didn't have that sort of connection with her past. She'd fallen out of touch with all her high school friends when she went out of state for college. And when she'd moved back after graduating, her college friendships faded away as well—or at the very least, had been reduced to texting and Facebook. Never in her adult life had Marina dropped by a friend's house for no other reason than to smoke a joint and shoot the breeze the way Matt and Evan did with Jason.

But now I have Morgan to drop by on, she reminded herself. Their new friendship wasn't quite like what Jason had with Evan and Matt, but it was growing. Although they still practiced softball—the impetus of their relationship—more and more of their time was spent just sitting around talking. It was fun, and it filled a hole in her life that she didn't realize how badly needed filling.

"Hey guys," Marina greeted the trio when she arrived at the house.

"Hey, how's it going?" Evan gave her a quick side-hug. "Where have you been lately? I feel like we never see you anymore."

"Her new 'BFF' Morgan's, I'd guess," Jason answered for her, exhaling a thin cloud of smoke.

"She's not my 'BFF,'" Marina said, taking the joint from Jason. "Just somebody I know from softball." She took a drag. Marina wasn't a big pot user but appreciated the occasional buzz.

"Yeah, right," Jason laughed. "You've been hanging out with her all the time, and you talk about her non-stop. If she's not your new BFF then she's your new *girlfriend*," he teased.

Marina shoved him. "Oh, shut up, you know it's not like that." Marina felt her cheeks burn and hoped that the guys were too high to notice.

"Is she hot, though?" Matt asked.

Jason fanned his face and batted his lashes. "Oh my God, guys. She's sooooo tall and strong," he said in an over-the-top falsetto imitation. "And her hair is so pretty it's like totally—"

"Shut up!" Marina shoved him again, and he started to laugh. The others laughed along with him, and Marina felt her cheeks burn hotter. She took another drag.

"You're so dumb, Jason," she huffed.

"So, she *is* hot," Matt said with a sideways grin. "Is she single?"

Marina nodded. The pot was mixing with the beer she'd had at Morgan's, making her light-headed and loopy. "Yeah, but you're not exactly her type," she said.

Matt straightened up. "Why? Is it a height thing? I am six feet tall, you know—"

"You wish," Evan snorted.

"No matter what these assholes tell you," Matt continued.

"You're five-eleven with heels on," Jason hooted. Matt shoved him, and the two began to grapple playfully.

Marina giggled as she pulled them apart. "Cut it out. It's not a height thing," she insisted.

"What is it then?" Matt asked, shooting Jason an I'll-get-you-next-time look.

"It's a penis thing," Marina said with a giggle.

"What? There's nothing wrong with my penis." Matt's hands went to the button of his jeans. "I can show you—"

"No!" the other three shouted in unison.

"She's a lesbian! Oh my God, keep that thing packed away," Marina said, putting her hand over her eyes.

"Ooh, well that explains it." Matt raised his hands and leaned back on the side of the house. "Since there's obviously no other reason why you wouldn't set me up with your hot friend."

Marina shook her head. "Oh, I can think of some reasons," she teased.

"Did you tell me she was a lesbian?" Jason asked, sounding a bit more sober than he had a minute ago.

Marina wasn't sure if she'd mentioned that fact about Morgan to him. "I don't see why it would matter," Marina said casually, flicking the spent joint onto the pavement. "It's not like I'm on the market anyway. Plus, she's out of my league. Girls like her don't look twice at girls like me."

Jason looked at her, his eyes shadowed under the light of the flood lamp. She couldn't read his expression and worried for a moment that he was actually upset that she'd been spending so much time with a single lesbian. But then Jason smiled. "Her loss, then," he said, throwing his arm around her shoulder. "Come on, mama, it's getting late." He turned to his buddies. "See you guys tomorrow, right?"

"Yup," Matt replied, handing Jason his empty beer can.

"See ya," Evan said as the two turned and stumbled down the driveway.

"You guys are walking, right?" Marina shouted after them; they were clearly too intoxicated to drive. Evan gave her a thumbs up.

"Walking to Mainstreet to hit the bar, that is," Matt called over his shoulder. "And *then* get a Lyft home," he added.

"Be safe," Marina called as the two disappeared into the dark. "Come on, Scout," Marina called to the sleepy pup as she let Jason lead her into the dark kitchen. She flipped on the light and dug through the pantry for a little bedtime treat for Scout. "You guys probably shouldn't smoke around the dog," she said.

"He was whining and scratching at the door to come out. What was I supposed to do?" Jason replied.

Marina shrugged. "Your dog." She looked at the side door; the once-white surface was a mess of paw prints and deep scratches. *I should do something about that.* She looked around her dingy little kitchen. *I should do something about a lot of things.* Her house always looked extra run-down after a day spent at Morgan's pristine home. "I could never invite Morgan over here," Marina mumbled, not really intending to say it out loud.

"Why's that?" Jason asked, reaching into the dated old fridge for another beer. He tossed one to her as well.

"Her place is just so damn perfect. It would be embarrassing," Marina said, taking a sip of the beer she most certainly did not need.

Jason put his arms around her waist from behind and rested his head on her shoulder. "If she's a real friend, she wouldn't judge. You think Evan or Matt give a shit what my house looks like?"

"It's not—" Marina stopped. She had almost said, "it's not your house," but that would have only started a fight, and she didn't want to fight. She was in a good mood. "It's not the same," she said instead. "You've known them forever. Plus, they're dudes."

"Yup, dudes with dicks that Morgan totally doesn't want," Jason said with a snicker. Marina rolled her eyes and took another sip. Behind her, Jason began to sway slightly, pressing against her. "You want this dick, though, don't you?" he whispered in her ear.

"Smooth," Marina said with a laugh. She finished off the beer. "Sure, why not."

"I feel so wanted," Jason said, feigning hurt.

Marina spun to face him. "Oh, yeah, baby, give it to me," she said dryly. "I'm so hot for you right now; I just can't stop." She looked him dead in the eye; there was a pause before they both broke into giggles. When their laughter faded, Marina took Jason by the hand and led him through to the bedroom. "Come on, if you really want sex you'd better hurry up and do me before I pass out."

"You're not going to get an argument from me," Jason let himself be led. "You know, I think we've been fucking more since you started hanging out with that Morgan chick."

"What?" Marina squinted at him as she began to undress.

Jason shrugged. "I'm not complaining. I'm just saying. We've totally been doing it more."

Marina considered this. *He's right, but it's got to be a coincidence. Doesn't it?* "Maybe when I have somebody to hang out with, I don't get pissy at you for spending all your time with the guys. Not being pissy is a pretty good aphrodisiac, right?"

Jason laughed. "Yeah, lack of annoyance is super sexy."

"No, *I'm* super sexy," Marina said, pulling off the last of her clothes and laying out on the bed, a sultry smile on her lips.

"Fuck yeah, you are," Jason agreed as he lowered himself down on top of her. For all his faults, Jason always managed to make her feel desirable. He may take for granted some of the things she did for him, like the housework or finances, but he never took her looks for granted. He made it clear that he felt like the lucky one—lucky to have a chance with a woman like her. Sometimes his constant horniness could be draining, but overall, it made Marina feel sexy.

Marina flipped him onto his back, taking charge. She liked the confidence she felt in the bedroom with him. *I would never be this confident with a woman.* The thought caught her by surprise. *Why am I thinking about being with a woman when I'm with Jason?* It was probably some combination of the conversation earlier with his friends and her own intoxication, but once the train of thought had begun, she couldn't stop it. *Women are so sexy.* In her mind, she could see the curves of a woman—her breasts, hips, thighs. Marina rode Jason hard as she imagined what it might be like to be in his position—laying prone with a sexy lady over her, watching her breasts bounce as she moved. Every time he touched her, it was like she was in his body, touching a woman she desired. The thought sent her over the edge, and she came hard, bringing Jason with her.

Later that night, while Jason slept beside her, Marina ran her fingers across the soft skin of her stomach, up to the curve of her breast. *What is it about boobs that's so alluring?* She pinched lightly at her own nipple. *I wonder what Morgan's boobs look like.* She froze, shocked at her own thoughts. *Go to sleep, Marina,* she told herself. She dropped her hand away from her breasts but slid the other down between her legs, lightly touching herself through her panties. She wondered if she could do all the things to another woman that she enjoyed having done to her. *As if I'll ever get the chance.* Her fingers brushed her clit, and even through the fabric, the touch was enough to make her breath catch. It was still sensitive from sex with Jason.

Jason. She thought about him, laying there beside her—about the enthusiasm with which he would touch her, how eager he always was to get his hands—or mouth—on her lady bits. *Would I feel the same enthusiasm if given the chance?* Marina's thoughts once more flicked unconsciously back to Morgan, and she snatched her hand away from her panties. *Nope, nope, nope. Can't think of that.* She flipped onto her stomach and squeezed her eyes shut. *Go to sleep,* she commanded herself once more. *That is no way to be thinking about a friend.*

Chapter 9
Morgan

Saturday morning, Morgan invited Kelly to meet her for coffee at a cute little bookstore and coffee shop a few blocks from her house. Kelly had gotten Morgan onto the Dirt Bunnies and into softball—a sport that she was growing fonder of by the day. Morgan owed her more than a casual conversation or two at their games.

Morgan paid for their drinks—over Kelly's objection—and the two stepped outside to sit on the shop's adorable little patio. The weather was fantastic. The sun was bright without being hot, and the sky was a blue so bright it hardly looked real. It was a perfect day for a latte outside with a friend.

"Thanks for meeting up with me," Morgan said, stirring her latte.

"Of course, thanks for the drink," Kelly replied, sipping her tea. "What's the occasion? Was there something you wanted to talk about?"

Morgan shook her head. "I just wanted to thank you for introducing me to the Dirt Bunnies."

"You're welcome." Kelly tilted her head.

"Besides, we haven't spent much time together lately, outside of softball," Morgan added.

"Yeah, no kidding. We miss you at summer hockey, you know," Kelly said.

"Do you really?" Morgan raised an eyebrow. She'd been under the impression that some of the summer hockey crowd didn't appreciate her presence. They liked to spend the summer dicking around on the ice— being silly and having fun but not *really* playing hockey. Morgan wasn't good at that "just have fun" style. She was too competitive.

Kelly shrugged. "I do, anyway. Why'd you decide not to play this year?"

"I have other things to focus on. The house, of course. But also, I'm really trying to get a better handle on softball. Marina's been helping me," Morgan said. Thinking about Marina invariably made her smile. They'd been getting so close lately, and Morgan liked that.

Kelly looked her over as she sipped her tea. "You and Marina have been spending a lot of time together, huh?" she asked, raising an eyebrow at Morgan.

"Yeah." Morgan sighed involuntarily. "She's great, isn't she?"

"Great and *straight*," Kelly said pointedly.

"No, she's bi," Morgan corrected, but Kelly only rolled her eyes. Morgan pursed her lips. She knew what Kelly was insinuating, and she didn't like it. "I do know she has a boyfriend if that's what you mean. I'm not trying to hit on her."

"Then what are you trying to do?" Kelly asked, resting her chin on her hand and looking at Morgan with skepticism.

"I *was* just trying to get better at softball," Morgan began.

"But now?" Kelly coaxed.

"I don't know. We're friends." Morgan shrugged and sat back. She didn't like feeling defensive about Marina. She wasn't pursuing Marina, but she really did like her. "We just get along so well. She's smart, and I don't say that about just anybody. Marina can keep all sorts of numbers in her head; it's pretty incredible. And she's funny too."

"So, you do have a crush on her," Kelly said, crossing her arms.

"No, I don't," Morgan replied. Kelly didn't say anything, just sat there giving her a discerning look until, with a groan, Morgan gave in. "Okay, fine. So, I have a *little teensy* crush on her."

Kelly dropped her arms and let out a long, exasperated sigh. "Why do you always do this to yourself, Morgan?"

"Why do I always do *what*?"

"Fall in love with totally unavailable women!" Kelly said as if it was as clear as the summer sky.

"I haven't fallen in love—" Morgan began to protest, but Kelly cut her off.

"I think it's a defense mechanism," she said, tapping her chin. "If you only let yourself catch feelings for women you can't get, then you never have to face *actual* rejection. You never risk getting your heart broken."

"That's patently absurd," Morgan protested with a snort.

"What's *absurd* is somebody like you being chronically single." Kelly gave her a look like a disapproving schoolteacher telling off a kid for poor behavior.

"What do you mean 'somebody like me?'" Morgan asked.

"Look at the facts." Kelly held up her index finger. "You're tall, blonde, and *gorgeous*. Your body is to die for—I'm insanely jealous, by the way—your skin is *perfect*," she said, counting her assets off one by one.

"I'm a dermatologist," Morgan protested.

"Yeah, exactly," Kelly threw her hands up she gestured at Morgan. "On top of being smoking hot you're also a fucking doctor! That means you're smart. And we both know you're a killer athlete. You're financially stable, socially approachable, confident, outgoing—"

"You have got to stop," Morgan said with a huff. She liked flattery as much as the next person, but this was getting ridiculous.

"My point, VanDolen, is that you're the whole package: beauty, brains, and brawn. There is absolutely no excuse for you to be single unless you're doing it on purpose." Kelly said it with such conviction—as if she were arguing that the earth was, in fact, round.

Still, Morgan didn't buy it. She blew a raspberry and shook her head. "Relationships don't work like that, you know," Morgan said. "There are two sides to finding somebody. A perfect resume means nothing if there aren't any good jobs open."

"So, you're saying nobody meets your standards?" Kelly asked.

"What? No. That's not what I…" Morgan sighed. "I just haven't found the right person at the right time."

"You'd have to look to find," Kelly said. Morgan opened her mouth to protest, but Kelly continued. "And by that, I mean look at girls who aren't already taken. Give somebody a chance."

Morgan sighed again and put her fingers on her temples. "Okay, fine. Do you have anyone in mind, or are you just having fun riding my ass?" Morgan asked.

Kelly smirked. "As a matter of fact, I do have somebody. Her name's Jenna. I'll give you her number."

This had been her goal all along. She'd raked Morgan over the you're-so-bad-at-dating coals just so that she could set her up with this Jenna chick. Morgan didn't love it, but at the same time, she had to begrudgingly admit that Kelly had made some fair points.

"Fine," Morgan agreed. "I'll go out with your friend."

"Good. I think you'll like her." Kelly grinned. "Maybe we'll run into her at Pride next week. Actually, that might be a good chance—"

Morgan shook her head. "I don't need you to arrange a meet-cute at Pride. I already said I'd call her. Will you drop it?"

"Consider it dropped." Kelly beamed at her.

Morgan sipped her latte for a bit as she tried to think of a new topic of conversation. "Have you noticed my batting average has improved?" Morgan asked. "I'm edging past Rebecca. My throwing's gotten better too."

Kelly rolled her eyes. "Is this 'stroke Morgan's ego' day or something?"

"Hey, I didn't ask you to say any of that other shit. If anything, I'd say you were—" Morgan stopped. Her conversation with Kelly was just making her crabby, and she had things she wanted to get done today before their game. "You know what, never mind. I have to get going anyway." Morgan moved to stand, but Kelly grabbed her wrist.

"Morgan, don't go," she said. "I'm sorry I was giving you a hard time."

"No, it's okay. I'm not mad; I'm just getting antsy." Morgan shook off Kelly's grip on her wrist and stood.

"I'm in the middle of demoing the back deck. If I want to get the new one built before the Fourth of July, I need to finish demo this weekend."

"You're building your own deck?" Kelly asked, standing as well. They moved to deposit their used mugs in the bus bin.

"Yes, I am," Morgan confirmed.

"Do you know how to do that?" Kelly asked, sounding skeptical. The pair stepped out onto the sidewalk.

"I've never done it before, but I'm confident I can figure it out. I am Morgan fucking VanDolen, after all." Morgan winked. "See you at the game, Kelly." With that, Morgan sauntered off toward home.

Morgan spent the afternoon in the yard, prying up lumber. The deck was so old and so poorly built that the boards came up easily. The whole project didn't take nearly as long as she'd been expecting. When she tossed the last piece into the dumpster, she still had an hour to spare before her softball game.

Morgan knew it didn't really make sense to shower *before* playing sports, but she was so sweaty and grimy that she took a quick one anyway. *At least I'll start the game looking presentable*, she thought as she pulled her long hair into its signature braid.

Morgan took her time, strolling casually to the park, yet was still early—the first to arrive. Not an unusual occurrence for her. *Fifteen minutes early is on time; on time is late; late is unacceptable.* She stretched as she waited for others to arrive. She could feel the toll of her earlier exertion in her arms and back. *Hopefully, all that physical labor on the deck doesn't impact my playing.*

"Hey, Morgan!"

A familiar voice broke Morgan from her thoughts. She turned to see Marina trotting up to her, hand-in-hand with her boyfriend.

"I don't think I've ever introduced you to Jason before," Marina chirped. "Jason, this is Morgan."

"Nice to meet you," Morgan said.

"So, you're renovating your house, huh?" He asked without preamble.

Morgan blinked. "Um, yeah. I pretty much gutted it and rebuilt the—."

"Marina's been going on and on about it," Jason interrupted. "She said you laid the floor and everything. Is that true?"

"Yes, I—" Morgan began.

"What kind?" Jason interrupted again.

Marina let go of Jason's hand, crossed her arms, and glared at her boyfriend. "Jason, you're being rude," she said sourly.

"You said you wished I could do the floors like Morgan, so let me find out how Morgan did it," Jason said.

Morgan was growing to actively dislike Jason. And not just because she was jealous that he was dating Marina. He was a total tool.

"So?" He looked expectantly at Morgan.

"Oak," Morgan answered, not sure what else she could do. The situation was odd and awkward. "I laid the click-and-lock style hardwood throughout the main level except for the bathroom where I did tile."

"Yeah? How'd it work out?" Jason crossed his arms and gave her a discerning look. "Was it hard to do?"

"Well, the wood wasn't too hard—"

"That's what she said," Jason snorted.

"As long as you measure carefully," Morgan continued. "The tile was a lot more tedious. I'm actually considering hiring somebody to it for the master bath. I certainly don't have the tile-laying skills of a professional."

"What you did looks so good, though," Marina said, beaming at Morgan. "All of it looks good. Those wood floors are *gorgeous*."

Jason didn't seem convinced. "Doing all that at once sounds expensive," he said.

"I budgeted for it when I bought the house," Morgan replied coolly. *As if it's any of your business.*

"You should have thought of that," Jason said, nudging Marina. Marina shot him a dirty look and muttered something under her breath, which he ignored. "I could give it a try, though," Jason continued. "Our house is dated as hell, isn't it, mama?" He nudged Marina again, but she stepped away from him. From the look on her face, Morgan would say Marina was pretty pissed off. Although Jason didn't seem to notice.

"We should go start warming up," Marina said, tugging at Morgan's arm.

Morgan waved goodbye to Jason as she let herself be led away. "What's got you all hot and bothered?" Morgan asked once they were safely out of earshot.

"Oh, it just gets under my skin the way he talks about 'our' house. It's *my* house." She shook herself off as if she could shake off her frustration like a dog shaking off water. "Whatever, it doesn't matter. Let's play ball."

Morgan couldn't help but notice that Marina continued to act as if something was on her mind. During the game, she kept glancing over at Jason in the stands. *Is she angry at him for how he talked about her house?* Marina didn't look angry, per se. She looked more unsure than anything.

"Are you okay?" Morgan asked her between innings as they picked up their gloves.

Marina started slightly. "What?"

"You seem distracted," Morgan said, looking inquisitively into Marina's big brown eyes. But she couldn't read anything specific in Marina's expression.

"I'm fine," Marina said with a small, unconvincing smile. She whacked Morgan on the arm. "What are you doing paying attention to me anyway? You're usually so hyper-focused on the game."

Morgan shrugged. "You've been teaching me that hyper-focus doesn't help me." She smiled at Marina. "I play better when I focus on *you*."

Marina's eyes widened, and her lips made a little surprised "O" shape. There was suddenly a charge in the air between them that made Morgan's pulse quicken.

"I, um," Marina stammered. She licked her lips. "You focus on… me?"

"I just mean, you're like my coach," Morgan amended quickly.

"Oh, yeah." Marina smiled and shook her head, her cheeks going pink. "That makes sense."

What was that? Morgan thought to herself as she took her place at first base. Morgan hadn't gotten that flirty vibe off Marina lately. They'd gotten so much closer as friends, but that's all it was: friendship. The little interaction they'd had just then somehow felt like more. *You're imagining it, VanDolen,* Morgan chastised herself. But it stuck in the forefront of her mind, and she played one of her best games of the season. *Being distracted by Marina really does work.*

Chapter 10
Marina

"Hey, Marina, are you going home with Jason, or are you going to hang out for a drink?" Morgan asked as they packed up their things. The game had gone very well; the Dirt Bunnies had crushed the other team. They would celebrate hard after that blow-out.

She looked from her teammates, gathering around Liz's car, to her boyfriend, waiting at the edge of the bleachers, then up at Morgan. She couldn't decide if she wanted to go home with Jason or hang out with her team. Neither seemed like exactly what she wanted. But what did she want?

"I'm going to go see what Jason wants to do," Marina told Morgan. Marina had realized that she didn't want to spend time with Jason and Morgan *together*. Everything about their earlier interaction had rubbed her the wrong way. Jason was on his worst behavior, and Morgan had acted oddly. *"I play better when I focus on you."* Marina shivered. Maybe it was her own imagination spinning stories born of the less-than-pure thoughts she'd had about Morgan the other night. Perhaps it was just a projection—a product of the guilt she felt over those thoughts. Whatever it was, things between her and Morgan felt different somehow.

"Hey, mama, good game." Jason kissed her cheek. "We taking off?" he asked, nodding his head in the direction of home. "Or do you want to hang out with your friends?"

"I honestly don't know," Marina confided.

"Why?"

Marina shrugged. "I'm in a weird mood today, I guess." She looked at her boyfriend. *Maybe he can make the choice for me.* "What do you want to do?" she asked.

"I don't know. Chill out?" Jason shrugged. "The guys were talking about coming over to watch the Twins' game." That made the decision a whole lot easier. It didn't take much for her to decern that she *wasn't* in the mood for hanging out with Jason and his buddies.

"Well, in that case, I guess I'll stick around here a bit longer," Marina said, tilting her head in the direction of the parking lot.

"Alright, see you at home." Jason planted a light kiss on her lips and turned to walk home. Marina made her way over to her teammates, standing in one large circle, clearly in the middle of a conversation.

"Hey, guys, what's up?" Marina asked, grabbing a beer and settling in.

"We're talking about Pride," Truck said. "That's coming up next weekend."

"Oh, yeah?" Marina said. She had mixed feelings about Pride.

"A group of us are going, apparently," Morgan said, smirking at Kelly before turning her gaze on Marina. "Would you like to join us?" she asked.

"Dude, she's not gay," Liz whispered, not quietly enough. Marina could hear her clear as day—as could the others who all turned to look at her.

"I thought you liked girls," Truck said, head tilted in question. "You're always eyeballing that chick from the Lions." She laughed, and Marina felt her cheeks go pink.

"I'm bi," Marina mumbled quietly, looking at her feet. *Why is saying that so hard?*

"Really? Have you ever *slept* with a woman? Like for real?" Liz asked, her eyebrow raised. *This is why.*

Marina looked down again. She hadn't ever slept with a woman and didn't want to have to admit that out loud to the whole team. She glanced at Jessica, who was giving her a sympathetic look. She was the only one on the team that knew Marina had never gotten past a PG-13 make-out session. *Will she say something?* The whole team was looking at her now, expecting her to say *something*. "It's… it's complicated," she mumbled.

Morgan silenced her with a wave. "You don't have to explain yourself. I think you should come with us," Morgan said, shooting Liz a not-so-subtle dirty look. The two often butted heads, and Marina could feel an air of anticipatory tension fall over the group.

Liz proceeded undeterred. "Yeah, but you have a boyfriend, right?"

Marina opened her mouth to answer, but Morgan jumped in before she had the chance. "What does that have anything to do with anything?" she asked, challenge in her voice.

Liz crossed her arms, unintimidated. "I'm just saying, she's living the straight life. She's got the privilege of passing as straight." Liz gestured at Marina, and Marina felt her cheeks and chest burn with embarrassment. "She's clearly never even had a real relationship with a woman," Liz continued. "She doesn't need Pride like we do."

Morgan narrowed her eyes and took a step toward Liz. "You're being an asshole," she hissed.

"No, it's okay," Marina found her voice. She tugged at Morgan's arm, pulling her away from their team manager. "Forget it, Morgan. I'm used to it. She's right. I don't really count."

"Like hell you don't," Morgan growled, her eyes still trained dangerously on Liz.

"You at least half-count," Truck said, wearing her let's-all-just-get-along grin.

Morgan's head whipped around so that her icy stare fell on Truck. "And saying that is only half as bad," she snapped.

"Oh, calm down," Kelly said, putting her arm around Truck and rolling her eyes at Morgan. "You're only getting your panties in a twist because you have a crush on her."

"Shut up," Morgan grumbled.

She does? Marina was conflicted on how she felt about that. It was flattering but also frightening. *Would Jason still be okay with me spending so much time with her if he knew she liked me?* Marina was pretty sure she knew the answer. *No way.*

Truck laughed. "Oooh… I see! You want to *turn* her," Truck cackled. "Well, that changes everything."

Liz scoffed. "It doesn't change anything. Morgan's little crush doesn't mean that Marina is actually interested in women," she said, digging her heels in on her opinion of Marina's sexuality. *Why the hell does she care so much?* Marina wondered.

"She is interested in women," Morgan crossed her arms. "She's just in a relationship with a man. For the time being." Morgan winked at Marina. That wink was like an electric shock, and Marina stepped back.

"I love my boyfriend, Morgan," she snapped. "So, no. I don't need to go to Pride. I've never felt like I belonged there anyway." She looked at Liz. "Thanks for reminding me." Marina tossed her nearly-full beer in the trash. "I'm out of here."

"Marina, wait," Morgan said, but Marina couldn't so much as look at Morgan. She folded her arms across her middle and walked faster.

"Hey, wait." Morgan jogged after her. "Marina. Come on. I was only trying to defend you."

"Defend me or get in my pants?" Marina looked at Morgan's face—at her memorizing blue eyes—and quickly looked away again. Her heart was beating out a frantic rhythm in her chest.

"That's not fair," Morgan said. "Come on, Marina. You're attractive, and you're cool. I'm sure I'm not the only girl to ever have a crush on you. That doesn't mean I ever expected anything to happen—"

"Good. Because it's not." Marina kept her face turned. She couldn't bear to look at Morgan. A voice inside her whispered, "what if?" But Marina wasn't about the give that thought purchase. *I have Jason. Jason loves me. I love him.*

"I know. I would never do anything to jeopardize our friendship," Morgan promised. "And I *don't* break up other people's relationships." Marina glanced back at her. Morgan's perfect lips were pressed together in a serious expression. *She means it.* It was both a relief and a disappointment at once.

"Thanks." Marina turned away again. "I just want to be alone now, okay?"

"Alright," Morgan acquiesced. "I'll see you at the next game?"

"Sure." Marina trudged home, tears trickling down her cheeks as she went. The worst part of it all was that, on some level, Marina knew Liz was right. She was in a heterosexual couple. If Jason were to ever propose, they could have a wedding her whole family would support. They could buy a house and have kids, and nobody would ever suspect that she was anything other than a "normal" wife. Marriage, kids—that was the life she'd always pictured for herself. So why did imagining her own wedding—one with Jason waiting for her at the alter—cause a painful knot form in the pit of her stomach? If she was happy in her relationship, why did seeing couples like Kelly and Truck fill her with jealousy? *They have something I'll never have, something I never gave myself the chance to have.* She couldn't decide who she was angrier at: Liz for calling her straight or herself for never having the guts to step outside of the safety of straight life.

By the time Marina got home, her tears were dry. And yet, Jason could tell something was wrong right away. He'd been sitting in the living room alone—no sign of his friends—drinking beer and watching baseball.

When Marina walked into the room, he turned off the TV. He looked her up and down. "What's up with you?" he asked.

"Nothing," Marina lied.

"Bullshit." Jason stood up. He moved to her, taking her face in his hands. "What's going on, mama?" he asked.

"I just…" Marina searched for words to explain her distraught appearance. "Some of the girls from softball were giving me a hard time about being bi." She wasn't about to mention the bit about Morgan's "crush." She still wasn't sure how she felt about that.

"What does that even matter anyway? You're with me, aren't you? Who even cares?" Jason replied with a scoff. It was a predictable reaction.

Marina slowly nodded her head. *It doesn't matter. It doesn't matter,* she repeated to herself. *It doesn't matter that I'm bi.* "You're right. Me being bi doesn't mean anything anyway. I'm with you."

"It means I get to take you with me to a strip club. That's something," Jason said with a wry grin.

"There is that." Marina let out a small, joyless laugh.

Jason kissed her. "Hey, I have an idea. Let's go put on some lesbian porn and fuck," he suggested, wiggling his eyebrows at her.

"Aren't the guys coming over?" Marina asked.

Jason shook his head. "Naw, they bitched out. So, what do you say?" he asked again, gesturing toward the bedroom. Marina wasn't exactly horny at the moment. Still, she liked sex, and it was always easier to agree than to turn him down. *Who knows, maybe I'll get in the mood.* That would be better than feeling the way she did.

"Sure." She let herself be led to the bedroom. *I wonder if lesbians watch lesbian porn.*

Later that night, Marina lay in bed, wide awake. The suggestion of porn and sex had been an utter failure. Marina just couldn't get into it. It all felt so fake. *Should I have liked the porn more?* Jason obviously liked it.

Beside her, he was sleeping soundly, his chest rising and falling in deep rhythmic breaths. Marina rolled to her back and looked up at the ceiling where she could just make out the moving shape of the spinning ceiling fan in the dim room. Her brain seemed to spin too, like the fan, stuck in one place going round and round in circles—constantly in motion but never getting anywhere. She could hear Liz's voice in her head: *"Have you ever slept with a woman? Like for real?"*

Thinking about it made Marina's chest tight and her throat burn. *Why do I have to be like this? What if I'm all torn up about being bi, and it's not even true? Liz is right; it's not as if I've ever had sex with a woman.* Although she'd kissed girls before, she'd usually needed the liquid courage of alcohol to do so. *Maybe I'm not bi and all. Maybe I just have some stupid need to feel special.* Tears blurred her vision, turning the ceiling fan into a watery blob. The tightness in her chest was starting to affect her breathing. *Am I really going to lay in bed crying over stupid internalized biphobic self-doubt?* She tried to scold herself out of crying, but the tightness only grew as the tears began to trickle from her eyes.

Marina bit her lip to keep from crying aloud as she quietly slipped out of bed. The last thing she needed was to wake Jason up with this nonsense. She slipped noiselessly from the room and padded softly into the kitchen. The linoleum floor was cold under her bare feet, and she shivered. Marina filled the kettle and put it on the stovetop to heat water for tea. She hugged herself as she waited. *How stupid am I to be losing sleep because of this?* Marina shook her head. Getting out of bed had lessened the tightness in her chest, but the stinging pain of self-doubt remained.

If Jason and I ever broke up, would I even have the courage to try dating women? Marina couldn't imagine what that would be like. Life wasn't a movie, this wasn't *But I'm a Cheerleader,* there was no Graham out there just waiting to take her hand and show her how queer she really was. Tears began to trickle down her cheeks again. *What if there is a woman out there who could love me? What if I never meet her because Jason found me first? Will I live my whole life, never really being certain that I am what I think I am?* Her silent tears became chest-sucking sobs, and she slumped into a kitchen chair and put her head in her hands. *It's not fair. I don't want to be like this. I never asked to be like this. Why can't I just let it go? I should just forget about it. Just be straight,* she commanded herself. *Everybody else thinks I might as well be straight, so just do it. Just be straight.* Her heart ached, and she knew it wasn't that easy.

"Hey, what's going on in here?" Jason's voice made Marina jump. She'd been so lost in her own self-pity that she hadn't heard him approach.

"You're up," Marina said, wiping tears from her eyes.

"A little hard to sleep with that." Jason pointed to the tea kettle, which was whistling shrilly.

Marina jumped up. She hadn't even noticed. *How self-absorbed am I?* "I'm sorry." She quickly switched off the stove and pulled the hot kettle from the burner. "I couldn't sleep, and I was making tea, but I was distracted—"

"It's okay," Jason said softly. He wrapped his arms around her. "Come here, mama. Tell me what's wrong."

"It's nothing," Marina sniffed as she nuzzled into his embrace.

"Like hell," Jason said. "You wouldn't be down here sobbing in the middle of the night over nothing. Come on, tell me."

Marina took a breath. "Remember earlier I told you some of the team was giving me a hard time for being bi?"

"Mm-hmm." Jason nodded, stroking her hair. "That's still bugging you?"

"It's not that exactly… it's just that… that what if they're right?" Marina could feel the sting of tears again. "I've never… I've never slept with a woman before. So how can I even say that I'm bi if I never…" She started to cry again.

"Come on, you can't let them get to you like this," he said in his most soothing voice. "I knew I liked girls before I'd ever actually gotten anywhere with one. What would make it different for you? I know you like chicks; you know you like chicks. Hell, you might be even more into tits than I am," he said with a chuckle.

"That's because you're an ass man," Marina said, smiling faintly and sniffing back her tears.

Jason put his hands on her ass and squeezed. "You got me there." He groped her ass for a bit before his hands began to wander. "Mmmm," he murmured as he touched her. "I like all parts of your body."

"Before you had sex, did you know you liked all the parts?" Marina asked.

"Huh?" Jason pulled back.

"Before you actually touched a woman's… you know… girl parts, were you sure you wanted to?" Marina asked.

"Are you asking if I knew I liked pussy?" Jason said, slipping one hand between her legs.

Marina nodded. "Yeah. I mean, beyond knowing you wanted to stick your dick in one."

"So, like, was I sure that I would want to do *this*?" he asked, sliding his hand inside her panties, fingering her gently.

Marina wouldn't have thought she would be in the mood, but as she imagined her own hand performing the same action on a woman, she started to feel the tickle of arousal. "Yes," she said, her voice coming out with a sigh. "Did you know you'd like doing this before you did it?"

"Honestly," Jason said as he continued to touch her. "I don't think I had a clue how much fun it would be to tease a woman… or make her wet."

Marina felt herself getting wet, half from his actions and half from the mental image of being in his place—of touching a woman, feeling her slick arousal. "God, I want to do that," she whispered.

"You want to finger-fuck a woman?" Jason asked, pushing his fingers inside of her.

"Yes," Marina breathed.

"Fuck, that's hot," Jason lifted her up onto the table and pulled down her panties. "And do you think you'd want to go down on her too?" he asked, kneeling so that he could bury his head between her legs.

"I don't know, I—" Marina gasped as he flicked his tongue against her clit. She let her head drop back as she thought about the question. She honestly couldn't envision what it would be like to go down on a woman. But she could easily picture a woman going down on her. When she closed her eyes, the view of Jason was replaced with images of a beautiful blonde-haired woman. *Morgan.* "Yes. Oh, God, yes."

As she grew closer to orgasm, Marina began to feel guilty. *Why am I doing this again? I shouldn't be thinking about her when I'm with him.* She opened her eyes, banishing visions of Morgan. Instead, she focused on Jason; she pulled him up and kissed him. "Fuck me," she demanded.

"Damn, if just thinking about banging a girl gets you this horny, maybe you should give it a go," he said with a grin. "The idea is certainly working for me."

"Just fuck me already," she said again, and he did—with gusto.

When they were done, Jason stepped outside to sit on the stoop and smoke a cigarette. Marina made herself a cup of lukewarm tea and joined him outside. The sun was just starting to peek above the horizon, and the sky was a beautiful blue-purple with the morning light.

Marina leaned her head against Jason's shoulder. "Did you mean what you said before?"

"When I said what?"

"That maybe I should try fucking a woman?" Marina asked with trepidation, her heart banging in her chest.

Jason shrugged. "I guess. I mean, as long as it's just sex. If it would make you stop doubting yourself so much." He looked at her and grinned. "And as long as you came home to me and told me all about it." She elbowed him. "What? It's hot!" he protested. He put out his cigarette and wrapped his arms around her. "Hey, mama. I'm serious. If you can find a chick out there willing to do you—no strings attached, knowing you've got a man at home—then I say do it."

"Really? You'd be okay with that?"

"For you, anything." He kissed the tip of her nose. "And if this woman wanted to come home and join *us* sometime…" He wiggled his eyebrows suggestively.

Marina rolled her eyes. She usually chastised him when he brought up threesomes; she'd told him plainly in the past that she wasn't interested. But she was too excited by the possibility before her. The chance to silence that doubting voice in her head once and for all.

Could there really be a woman out there who would do that for me? She wondered. Despite where her imagination had gone before, she knew it could never be Morgan. It wouldn't be just sex with her; Marina cared about her too much to risk ruining their friendship. If it was going to work, it would have to be with somebody who could separate sex and relationships. *Maybe I should talk to Jessica.*

Chapter 11

Morgan

It had been difficult for Morgan to watch Marina walk away after their last game—aware of how hurt she was. She had been Morgan's best friend these last couple of months, and she didn't want to lose that.

Morgan texted Marina first thing the following day, even before she'd had her coffee. "Hey, I'm sorry about yesterday, both about what Liz said and my own part in making things uncomfortable. I hope you're doing okay."

Marina didn't text back. Morgan left for work with an uncomfortable tightness in her chest. She'd known that Marina's friendship was important to her, but she hadn't realized how deep her feelings ran until that friendship was threatened. She'd never felt such bone-deep anxiety over losing a friend before. And she'd only met Marina a few months ago.

Morgan didn't like having her personal phone with her when she worked. Giving patients her complete focus was critical. That personal attention was the cornerstone of her business. Insurance didn't always cover dermatological issues, but people paid out of pocket to see her because she was good at her job. Today Morgan made an exception. When she still hadn't heard from Marina by lunch, Morgan swallowed her pride and sent one more text. "Are we okay?"

This time Marina responded right away. "OMG I'm sorry. I saw your last text on my way to work and then totally spaced. Yes, we're okay."

Morgan let out a breath in relief. "I'm glad. Your friendship is important to me. How are you doing?" she texted back.

"I'm fine."

Fine didn't have the strongest positive connotation. Especially coming from a girl. After a pause, Morgan texted back. "Are you still upset about what Liz said?"

"Yes and no. It still bothers me but I had a good chat with Jason and he made me feel better."

Jealousy pricked at Morgan. She knew it wasn't fair, but she wished she could have been the one to make Marina feel better. *Instead, I made it worse. I should be glad she has a partner who can help her like that.*

"That's good," Morgan replied. "You want to hang out tonight?"

"I can't, sorry. Busy week."

Morgan wondered what Marina could have going on that made it a busy week. Maybe something with Jason? Or work? Morgan hoped she was honestly busy and not making an excuse to avoid her. "But I'll see you at the next game?" Morgan asked.

"Of course!" Marina replied almost instantly.

Morgan typed out another text: "Maybe we could do a practice and pizza kind of thing after?" *You are starting to sound desperate, VanDolen,* she scolded herself. But she sent the message anyway.

"Maybe! I might have something going on but if not I'm totally there," came Marina's cryptic reply. Morgan wanted to ask what she might have going on, but she felt like she'd been clingy enough for one day. Besides which she was going to be late for her next appointment.

"Cool, see you then!" Morgan texted back, left her phone at her desk, and returned to work.

The four-day wait until the Dirt Bunnies' next match-up crawled by. When the day came, Morgan left for the park as early as was passably reasonable. She was surprised to see Marina already there when she arrived. And even more surprised to find her warming up for the game with Jessica. They were the only ones on the field.

"Hey, you're early for once in your life," Morgan teased as she joined them.

"Oh, yeah, well, uh," Marina stammered, visibly flustered. "Jessica and I were, uh…"

"We're doing a little bisexual buddy system," Jessica jumped in. "After what Liz said, Marina needed a little bi-buddy-backup." She winked at Marina, and Marina's face went pink.

Morgan wasn't exactly sure what Jessica meant, but it was good that Jessica had Marina's back. It was too bad she hadn't been there the other day; maybe then Marina would have had "backup" she appreciated. And given that Jessica was with a woman, Liz might have even taken her seriously.

Morgan glanced around. There was no sign of Jessica's girlfriend today. "Where's Cassie?" Morgan asked. It was unusual for her to miss a game.

Jessica waved her hand dismissively. "I sent her off on a camping trip with some of my buddies. So, she's… tied up at the moment." She smirked. "Anyway, here."

She tossed Morgan the ball. "I'm warmed up enough, and I have a few words for Liz." Jessica sauntered off.

Morgan turned to Marina; she was watching Jessica walk away, an odd look on her face.

"Are you okay?" Morgan asked, and Marina started.

"What? Oh, yeah." Marina took a deep breath and smiled. "I'm not quite sure what Jessica is going to say to Liz, but I appreciate her support."

"I support you too," Morgan blurted out without thinking.

Marina looked at her, and her smile softened. "I know, Morgan. I appreciate that too." She pounded a fist into her glove. "Now come on, give me some of those wild VanDolen throws."

Morgan laughed. "They aren't as wild as they once were, you know," she said.

"Prove it," Marina said, and Morgan threw the ball. It flew fast and *almost* on target. Marina was forced to move, but she caught it easily. "Not bad. Maybe the practice is paying off. Although there's still room for improvement."

Morgan liked how Marina could be honest with her about her skills now. It was incredibly helpful. "Are you up for a little practice after the game?" Morgan asked as she caught the ball Marina tossed back.

"No, I'm sorry, but I have, uh, plans," Marina said, glancing furtively toward the dugout.

Morgan frowned. *I thought we were good. If we're okay, why is she acting so weird today?*

"I'm sorry," Marina repeated.

Morgan shook her head, shaking off the disappointment, and grinned at Marina. "No worries. Maybe I'll crack out that pitching machine again. It's been a while."

"Or maybe you'll hit so many pitches during the game you won't need any more practice," Marina said.

"Fat chance." Morgan had admitted that thinking about Marina could distract her into a good game, but this wasn't the same. She'd been so worried about having damaged their friendship she was in an entirely different mind-space. *I need to shake it off.* "We are still okay, right?" Morgan asked.

"Of course," Marina assured her. But still, Morgan felt like something was off. In fact, the whole dynamic of the team felt off. There was an awkward tension in the dugout. Despite her reassurances, Marina seemed a little detached. As if her mind were somewhere else. She dropped balls, struck out, and made uncharacteristically bad plays. As she had predicted, Morgan didn't have her best game either. Nobody did. They lost the game by a six-run margin.

Morgan walked home after the game, kicking at the ground as she went. She didn't like losing, she didn't like how she'd played, and she hated that the tension on the team had kept most people—including herself—from hanging out after the game.

Morgan took the long route home, hoping the walk would make her feel better. It did not. When she got back to her house, she dug the pitching machine out of her garage. She hadn't used it much since she'd started practicing with Marina. But Marina wasn't available today, and Morgan wanted to do something to make up for that mess of a game.

She loaded the machine into her jeep and drove back to the park, crossing her fingers that the batting cages would be free. When she got there, the whole place looked empty. Slinging her duffle bag across her back and hefting the heavy machine in her arms, Morgan waddled down the cement path between the two fields and toward the batting cages. She was about halfway there when she spotted two figures around the back of the concession stand, pressed together against the wall. It was two women, a blonde and a brunette of approximately equal height. They were engaged in some pretty serious kissing. When Morgan got close enough to recognize them, she stopped dead, nearly dropping the machine.

Marina and Jessica? She blinked a few times, but her eyes weren't deceiving her. Petite beautiful Marina was lip-locked with bold, buxom Jessica, whose hands were roaming Marina's body hungrily. *What is Jessica doing to her?* Morgan couldn't believe that Marina would honestly be interested in Jessica, of all people. But there she was, kissing her back and grabbing at her t-shirt like she wanted to rip it off. A cold wave of jealousy washed over Morgan. *She said she couldn't be with me because she was with Jason. So, what the hell is this then? Is this why things were so awkward today? What about Jessica's girlfriend?* It honestly didn't seem out of character for Jessica to be cheating—she flirted with just about everything on two legs. But Marina wasn't like that. At least Morgan hadn't thought so.

The kissing slowed, and they parted. Morgan ducked behind the batting cages, her heart hammering, hoping they hadn't spotted her. As softly as possible, she set down the pitching machine. She risked a peek back at the two.

Jessica said something that Morgan couldn't make out, and Marina nodded. Taking her by the hand, Jessica turned and led Marina away from the ballpark. They crossed the street and got into Jessica's car together. A thunderstorm of emotion rumbled in her chest as Morgan watched them drive away. Confusion, anger, jealousy, and most acutely: hurt.

There were tears in her eyes, but VanDolens didn't cry, so Morgan gritted her teeth and kept them in check. With Jessica and Marina gone, Morgan stepped out of her hiding spot. She ripped open her bag, pulled out her bat, and stepped into the batting cage. Morgan often dealt with her feelings by shooting hockey pucks. There was no better medicine for unwanted emotions than taking a few good hard swings at something. *Hitting balls is almost the same as hitting pucks*, she reasoned. That's why she'd come to the park in the first place, wasn't it? To work out her frustrations?

But these feelings were beyond frustration, and, as it turned out, batting *wasn't* just as good at shooting. When Morgan shot pucks, she hardly ever missed the net, and she never missed the puck itself. Making contact with a moving softball wasn't as easy. And without the cathartic sensation of making contact, Morgan's emotions didn't fade. With each miss, the pain of those unwanted feelings grew sharper. It was hard to keep her eye on the ball when all she could see was the vision of Marina kissing Jessica. Beautiful, voluptuous Jessica, with her pouting lips, perfect make-up, and sexy clothes. Jessica, who always had an easy smile for everybody, who could flirt her way to free drinks at any bar—gay or straight. *Is that the kind of woman Marina is into?*

Morgan had a high opinion of her looks. As much as she wouldn't have said so outright, she'd agreed with Kelly's assessment: she was a catch. And yet she knew she couldn't compete with that level of flirty, feminine charm. If that's what Marina was into, she'd never had a chance to begin with. Morgan swung the bat. Another miss. She cursed and threw the bat against the side of the cage; it clattered against the fencing before falling to the dirt.

Jessica is better at this stupid sport than me too. Jessica didn't even seem to *care* about softball. She could giggle and wave to her girlfriend even as their team got slaughtered. In fact, Jessica only seemed to play softball to show off for her girlfriend—a girlfriend she was willing to cheat on right there in the same ballpark. *What the fuck does Marina see in her?*

Morgan wasn't sure how she would be able to look Marina in the eye again after seeing what she'd seen. Morgan hated how jealous this was making her. It wasn't like her. She hated it. And at the moment, she kind of hated softball too. She packed up her things and threw them into her jeep. *I should never have agreed to play on this stupid team.*

Chapter 12
Marina

Marina was shaking like a leaf as Jessica unlocked her townhouse door and flipped on the lights. The townhouse was decorated in shades of gray with the occasional pop of red. It looked like a showpiece—more of a statement than a home. Marina wondered how many women Jessica had brought back here. Women who were there for the same reason she was: sex. No-strings-attached, just-for-fun, girl-on-girl action. Jessica was experienced in this realm. Marina was not. *Jessica knows that; that's why I asked her. It's okay,* Marina reassured herself.

"Are you alright?" Jessica asked, putting her hands on Marina's hips and drawing her close.

"Yeah, I'm good," Marina pulled Jessica's head in close and kissed her with a boldness that surprised herself. "Great, even." This is what she wanted, and she wasn't about to back down. But that didn't mean she wasn't nervous as hell.

"Okay then," Jessica replied with a grin. "The bedroom's just up the stairs."

"Lead the way," Marina said with a nod. "And you're sure Cassie is okay with this?" Marina added as they ascended the stairs. She knew Jessica and Cassie were non-monogamous—that's what made Marina approach her in the first place. And Jessica had assured her that meant there would be no hard feelings or complications. But Marina still felt compelled to confirm it once more before clothes came off and they hit the point of no return.

"Yup! She thinks it's really cool that you came to me with your little hall-pass situation," Jessica said as they stepped into the bedroom.

"Hall pass?" Marina repeated.

"You know, your boyfriend giving you a pass to sleep with a woman, just the once." She looked Marina straight in the eye. "That's what this is, right? No relationship, no expectations, just sex?"

"Yes, right. Exactly." Marina nodded, although hearing the word *sex* come from Jessica's full lips had set Marina's heartbeat racing. *Just sex. With a woman.*

"Great," Jessica said, pulling her shirt and bra up and over her head, exposing her large, round breasts and perky pink nipples.

Through her nervousness, Marina felt a jolt of arousal. Her mouth watered at the sight of Jessica's bare chest. She pulled Jessica close and kissed her. Jessica's kisses were so different from Jason's. The way she used her tongue and the plumpness of her lips all made the whole experience entirely unique and incredibly pleasant. As they kissed, Marina put one trembling hand on Jessica's breast. She could feel Jessica's nipple against her palm, and her arousal grew.

"Mmmm," Jessica moaned, putting her hand atop Marina's and pressing it tighter against her chest. "Don't be gentle," she said in a throaty whisper. Marina squeezed hard, and Jessica sighed encouragingly. Marina lifted her hand so that she could pinch Jessica's nipple, and Jessica's head fell back with another pleasure-filled sigh. Emboldened, Marina grabbed Jessica's other breast in her left hand before dipping her head and covering Jessica's nipple with her mouth. She flicked the nipple with her tongue.

"Oh, yeah," Jessica moaned, her hand coming to rest on the back of Marina's head.

Marina's tongue flicked back and forth across Jessica's nipple. The sensation of having her mouth on Jessica was creating a flood of wetness between Marina's legs. She lightly nipped at Jessica's nipple with her teeth, and the grip Jessica had on her head tightened.

"Oh, fuck, yeah," Jessica groaned. "God, I need you." She pulled Marina's head away from her chest. "Get naked," she commanded, and Marina didn't hesitate to obey. She stripped off her t-shirt, shorts, and panties as Jessica removed the remainder of her own clothing. Then Jessica pushed her down onto the bed. Before Marina really knew what was going on, Jessica was on top of her. Jessica's mouth went to one of Marina's small breasts while her hand roamed first across Marina's chest to pinch at her other nipple, then down between her legs. Marina let Jessica part her thighs just enough to slide her hand between them.

"Oh God, you are so wet," Jessica purred as her fingers found Marina's slit. Marina moaned, her hips squirming as Jessica ran her fingers gently along the edge of her opening, up to her clit, and back down again. She pushed her fingers inside, and Marina arched her back, letting out another primal groan of pleasure.

Jessica worked her fingers in and out until Marina was panting. Suddenly she pulled her fingers away. Marina whimpered, but Jessica hushed her.

"Trust me." She moved to straddle Marina, their legs intertwined, their bodies lined up just right so that Jessica could press her wet mound down against Marina's.

Oh my God, this is it, Marina thought. *This is what it's like to have sex with a girl.* It felt pretty fucking good. Jessica leaned down to kiss her as she began to move her body against Marina's rhythmically. The sounds their bodies made as they pressed together weren't particularly sexy. But the feeling and the view more than made up for the sounds. Marina looked up at Jessica in awe as the sexy blonde rode her—her breasts swaying with each roll of her hips. Marina watched her, entranced as Jessica shuddered and came, groaning and twitching with pleasure. It was a beautiful image.

As Jessica slid down and away from her previous position, Marina worried it might be over. Although it had been fun, Marina wasn't ready for it to be over. She wanted more; she wanted the chance for her own orgasm. But her concerns were quickly calmed; Jessica didn't quit. She wrapped her arms around Marina and rolled beneath her.

"Ride me," she whispered, her voice breathless and husky. Marina didn't fully understand what that meant. She did her best to imitate the position and movements that Jessica had been doing. Her awkwardness must have been apparent because Jessica put her hands on Marina's hips and slowed her movements with a slight shushing sound. "Just find what feels good to you," she instructed. "Don't worry about me."

Marina nodded, but she couldn't calm her nerves enough to figure out what felt good. It had seemed so easy when Jessica was on top. Jessica pulled her down and kissed her. That helped. Jessica's kisses redirected Marina's mind away from her body. Jessica squirmed beneath her as they kissed, and Marina felt something hard rubbing against her clit. *Jessica's hip bone.* It felt good. Soon it felt so good that Marina could no longer focus on kissing. When she came, it was like the bursting of a damn. Any tension left in her body melted away under the release.

Jessica was still moving beneath her, her breathing shallow. Marina continued to press her body down against Jessica's, caressing Jessica's breasts with her mouth and fingers. Her actions were met with moans of encouragement. Jessica pushed her hips up hard against Marina, increasing the pace of her movements.

"Bite my nipple," Jessica demanded. Marina nipped at it cautiously. "Oh, God, yes." Jessica tightened her grip on her. Marina could feel the heat between her legs growing again as she used her teeth and tongue on Jessica. It was incredible how arousing the action was. *I really am bi. Oh my God. It's really true. I* like *this.* By the time Jessica came again Marina was back to writhing in desire.

"Mmmm, that was good," Jessica purred. She kissed Marina. "You're fun when you let go." She grinned at Marina as she slid out from beneath her and rolled Marina to her back. "Now, just lay back and relax."

"What?" Marina asked, a little whine in her voice as her body protested the loss of sin-on-skin contact with Jessica.

"May I go down on you?" Jessica asked and Marina nodded without hesitation. When Jessica's mouth made contact, Marina rolled her head back and sighed. Jessica's tongue was like magic on Marina's aching clit. It took very little time for the heat within her to build to a crest. Marina came with a gasping scream. When

Jessica lifted her head, Marina shut her legs tight together and rolled to her side, her body twitching with the aftershocks of orgasm.

"Oh fuck," she whispered as she caught her breath. "That was amazing."

"It was over so quick, I barely got to taste you," Jessica said, a playful pout in her voice. She came up behind Marina and spooned her. "I'm glad you had fun," she said, her breath hot in Marina's ear.

"Did you?" Marina asked, suddenly nervous for the answer. *Did I do okay? She did so much more than me.*

But Jessica laughed. "Of course!" she said, squeezing Marina tightly. "Didn't I sound like I was having fun?" she teased.

"Yeah, that was one of the best parts." Marina smiled to herself. "Thank you."

"Did you get out of the experience what you wanted?" Jessica asked.

Marina nodded. "Yeah, I think I did."

"Good." Jessica nuzzled closer to her. "Do you want to stick around to cuddle, or do you have to get home to your man?"

"I should probably get going," Marina said. The sex had been great but cuddling felt intimate in a way that she wasn't sure was included in this "hall pass" situation. "Sorry," she said, rolling away from Jessica and standing up.

"Nothing to be sorry for," Jessica replied, laying on her side and watching as Marina pulled on her clothes. "Like I said, I had fun."

Marina finished dressing. "So, I guess I'll see you at softball?"

"Here, I'll walk you out." Jessica popped out of bed. She didn't bother with clothes. "You were a bit distracted when we got here; I'd hate for you to get lost. Not that my place is that big." Jessica tittered.

"Thank you," Marina said. "For everything."

"Any time." Jessica gave her a quick squeeze before Marina turned and walked out, shutting the door—quite literally—on her first time with a woman.

Jason was waiting for her when she got home. "So, did you fuck that girl?" he asked just about the second she stepped into the living room.

"Yes, we had sex," Marina said, sitting down next to him on the sofa.

"Well?" Jason coaxed when she didn't offer any follow-up. "What was it like?"

"It was… good. I'm pretty sure I'm definitely bi now." Marina put her hand over Jason's and smiled at him. "Thank you so much for letting me do that. I think it really helped."

"Good." Jason kissed her on the forehead. "Now tell me *everything*."

Marina did her best to recount the encounter. It was a little awkward; she didn't feel like she had all the correct vocabulary. She ended up doing a lot of crude imitations of their limbs with her fingers. She'd gotten Jessica's permission to share all the details, and she was glad she had because Jason was *really* excited to hear them.

"So, she went down on you, but you didn't go down on her?" he asked when she was done. He sounded disappointed.

"Uh, yeah." Marina hadn't really thought of it like that exactly. Their stopping point had felt so natural. *Should I have offered?*

"I guess it still counts as sex," Jason concluded with a shrug.

Does it? Marina was suddenly unsure. She was unsure as to what exactly constituted "sex" between two girls. Did she meet the threshold even without giving her oral? *I didn't finger her either.* "I probably should have done more," she said, feeling suddenly deflated about the whole experience. She had been so nervous going in, she'd just followed Jessica's lead. *This was my one chance, and I missed out on so much.* Marina suddenly felt near tears.

"Don't worry, mama," Jason said, kissing her lightly. "If you want, you can do that during the threesome."

Marina started. "The what? What threesome?"

"You know. You, me, and this Jessica chick," Jason said as if this should have been obvious.

"Huh?" Marina sat back, her disappointment replaced with confusion.

"Oh, come on," Jason looked honestly surprised by her reaction. "This was *totally* an experiment to lead up to a threesome."

"No, it wasn't," Marina said, shocked. "I never said… there was no plan to—"

"Isn't Jessica into that sort of thing?" he asked. "From what you told me, she sounded like she'd be down."

"I don't…" Marina didn't have words. Sure, Jessica *might* be into that sort of thing, but it had never been something Marina wanted. She'd said as much many times in the past. She'd assumed he knew that sleeping with Jessica wouldn't change that. But the way Jason talked turned that assumption upside-down.

Jason reached out a hand and stroked her cheek. "It's okay. If she's not into it, I'm sure we can find a girl who is," he said in a soft tone. *He thinks he's being comforting.* If so, he didn't understand her reaction at all.

"But *I'm* not into it!" Marina said firmly, pulling away from his touch.

Jason looked perplexed. "What do you mean, you're not into it? You said you liked fucking her," he said.

"I did but—" Marina began.

"And you still like fucking me, right?" Jason interrupted.

"Yeah, but—" She tried again.

"So now you know you're definitely bi then," he continued.

"That doesn't mean I want a threesome!" Marina snapped, finally getting out a complete sentence.

Jason stared at her like she'd just declared she was giving up oxygen for lent. "I don't understand."

"Clearly," Marina huffed.

"What's the point of being bi if—" he began.

"Point?" Marina shrieked. "There's no *point* to being bi, Jason. It's just what I am!" Marina stared back at him, incredulous. *He doesn't really believe that, does he?* She didn't want to think that her boyfriend—the man she'd chosen to be with—would genuinely believe that she would have threesomes just because she was bisexual.

"I'm sorry," Jason said.

There was a long silence as Marina tried to wrap her mind around what he'd said. She wasn't even done processing what she'd just done; no part of her was prepared to discuss a threesome.

Jason squirmed in his seat. "Look, I don't want to fight about this. I'm glad you had fun, and we can talk about the threesome another time." He leaned forward and touched her face again. "Right now, I'm just really turned on, thinking about you with a woman."

"I'm not going to sleep with her again," Marina insisted. "It was a one-time thing."

"Sure, it was," Jason said as if he didn't believe a word of it. He stood and extended his hand. "Come on, let's take a break from talking and spend some time making sure you still like men." He wiggled his eyes suggestively at her.

Hesitantly she allowed herself to be pulled to standing. *The threesome idea is just a fantasy. I knew he liked girl-on-girl stuff. I should have expected the question; that doesn't mean he really thinks it's going to happen.* Marina worked hard to reassure herself. It was the only thing that made sense. *It's just a fantasy,* she repeated. *We all have fantasies. And I got to live one of mine today.* Marina thought of Jessica and of what they'd done. She felt the residual heat and excitement from that encounter. "Yeah, okay, let's go." Marina agreed and followed Jason to the bedroom.

Chapter 13

Morgan

Morgan was surprised when Marina texted her the next day and asked her to hang out as if nothing unusual had happened. Morgan did want to spend time with her, but at the same time, she was still reeling from what she'd seen back at the ballpark. She wasn't sure she'd be able to act as if she hadn't seen what she had. *Maybe she'll tell me.* They told each other things; Marina was a sexual person and often talked about her relationship with Jason. She told her about the time he had insisted on doing it while watching lesbian porn. Marina had asked if she, as a lesbian, liked lesbian porn. Morgan did not. *If she can ask me about that, she can tell me about this.*

But when Marina arrived, she didn't say a word about Jessica. Morgan gave her several openings, bringing up Jessica casually in conversation, remarking on her own lack of a girlfriend. She told Marina about the pointless blind date Kelly had set up for her. It had not gone well. The woman had gone in for a kiss, but it was cold and awkward—*nothing* like the kiss Morgan had witnessed between Marina and Jessica. When the story of her fruitless date failed to get Marina talking, Morgan decided on a more direct approach.

They were just tucking into their dinner of delivery hamburgers and fries when Morgan cleared her throat. "So," she said, taking a deep breath and trying to act as if the topic she was about to broach didn't make her wildly uncomfortable. "What's the deal with you and Jessica?"

"What?" Marina's head shot up. She nearly choked on her burger. "What about me and Jessica?"

"I saw you making out at the field," Morgan admitted. The look on Marina's face was of unmasked shock and embarrassment. Morgan grimaced. "I'm sorry, was it a secret? I figured since you were out in public…" she trailed off.

The shock faded from Marina's face, but she was still clearly embarrassed; her shoulders slumped, and she let out a long sigh. "Yeah, I guess we should have been more discreet. Do you know if anybody else saw?"

Morgan shook her head. "I don't think so. I was the only one there that I could see."

"Good." Marina went back to her hamburger, but Morgan was far from satisfied.

"So, I take it you're not officially seeing each other then?" she said. She wondered if they were hiding the affair from Jessica's girlfriend or Jason or both.

"No," Marina said through a mouthful of food. "It was a one-time thing." She swallowed. "And before you ask, Jason is aware that I slept with her—"

"You *slept* with her?" Morgan shrieked a bit too forcefully.

"—and he's fine with it," Marina finished, scowling.

Morgan squinted at Marina. "Really?"

Marina's expression didn't change. "Yes. He is," she replied, her voice cool.

"And what about Jessica's girlfriend?" Morgan pressed. She didn't like how adversarial the conversation felt. At the same time, she wanted to get to the bottom of whatever the hell was going on.

Marina wrinkled her nose. "Cassie? What about her?"

"Are she and Jessica pretty serious? It seems like they—"

"It's fine, really," Marina said, flicking her wrist dismissively. She leaned back and picked up a French fry. There was visible tension in her jaw as she chewed. "They're non-monogamous."

"Non-monogamous?" Morgan repeated.

"They both sleep with other people," Marina explained, her tone cold and condescending.

"I understand what non-monogamous means." Morgan tried to keep the bite out of her voice. She wasn't angry with Marina; she was *worried* about her. She didn't understand why she would do something that seemed so out of character like this. *Maybe I don't know her as well as I thought I did.* "Are you and Jason non-monogamous?"

"No. Like I said, this was a one-time thing. Like a 'hall-pass' situation," said Marina.

"But doesn't he—" Morgan began.

"For your information, it was basically his idea," Marina interrupted sourly.

Morgan really didn't understand that. What would make a guy want his girlfriend to sleep with somebody else? Didn't he get jealous? In the brief time she'd met him, Morgan had pegged him as the possessive type. Her impression didn't fit this reality. *What is he getting out of it?* "Did he watch?"

"What? No!" Marina yelped, her mouth dropping open.

"Well, why would he want you to?" Morgan asked.

"Because *I* wanted to, Morgan," Marina snapped. "He was being supportive."

"I'm sorry. I didn't mean to…" Morgan pressed her lips together. "Why did you want to?"

Marina looked away—as if she couldn't both look Morgan in the eye and answer the question. "I just want to… to make sure," she said.

"To make sure of what?" Morgan asked.

"That I'm really bi," Marina answered, her voice wavering ever so slightly.

"I thought you realized you were bi back in high school," Morgan said.

"I did."

"So, then why did you need to sleep with Jessica?"

"Because I'd never slept with a woman before," Marina grumbled, still unable or unwilling to meet Morgan's eye. She snorted. "I'd barely done anything. Just making out. Nothing naked. Nothing 'below the belt.' I'd always thought… but I didn't *know*. I wanted to know. I wanted to finally prove that I really am what I thought I was."

"Prove it to whom?" Morgan asked.

"To myself, okay?" Marina snapped, finally turning to look at Morgan. "To me and to everybody. Nobody ever takes me seriously. You heard Liz. I already 'don't count' because I'm dating a guy. When people find out I never even slept with a woman—"

"Why would they ever have to find out?" Morgan broke in.

Marina *glared* at her. "Do you have any idea how often I get asked to prove my queer cred? All the fucking time." Marina stood up and began to pace the kitchen. "It's invasive and stupid, but it happens. And I was sick to death of evading questions or being vague. Hell, I've outright lied before, just because I was too embarrassed to admit what I'd never done."

"But you shouldn't need to prove who you are to *anybody*," Morgan put extra effort into keeping her voice calm, hoping to soothe some of Marina's agitation.

Marina stopped pacing and looked directly at Morgan. "But I did," she said. She swallowed audibly, and Morgan wondered if she was going to cry. Marina's eyes seemed to shimmer as she spoke. "Because all those comments, all those questions—over and over my whole adult life—made me question *myself*. I felt like a fraud. I needed to prove it to *me*." Marina pressed her index finger to her chest. Morgan could see that her hands were shaking.

"I guess I can appreciate that," Morgan said, although she didn't fully understand. She'd known she was gay for years before she'd ever had sex, and nobody would have been able to tell her otherwise. "But what I don't get is why you decided sleeping with *Jessica* was the best way to do that."

"Don't judge me, Morgan," Marina croaked.

"I'm not judging; I'm just concerned. Jessica is kind of..." Morgan winced. "I don't want to say slutty, but—"

"Yeah, she's slutty. So what?" Marina crossed her arms. "That's why I picked her. It was a sure thing. And she's bi too, so she—"

"Have you gotten tested?" Morgan asked.

Marina started, clearly surprised by the forwardness of the question. "No, not yet, but she said she just did."

"You need to get tested," Morgan insisted. "If you *really* had sex with her—"

"What do you mean 'really'? Oh my God, do you want me to tell you what we did? Do you need a play-by-play so you can decide if I 'really' had sex with her?" Marina threw up her hands and began to pace again. "Jesus, Morgan! You're just like all the rest of them!"

"That's not what I meant," Morgan insisted. "I just want to make sure you're being safe."

"It's none of your business," Marina growled.

"Well, I'm making it my business," Morgan said, undeterred. "Because you're my friend and I care."

"You mean because you have a *crush* on me," Marina snapped, narrowing her eyes on Morgan. "And you're angry because I didn't choose *you* to sleep with."

Morgan felt her face burn. She looked away; now, she was the one unable to look her friend in the eye. She was ashamed of the truth she knew Marina's remark contained. She hadn't consciously meant to push Marina out of jealousy, but that didn't mean it hadn't played a part in her reaction to the situation.

"I'm sorry," Marina said, her voice soft and quiet, her anger suddenly gone. "I shouldn't have thrown that back at you like that."

Morgan looked up into Marina's beautiful face. She was looking at her with such tenderness. It made Morgan feel even worse for having acted from a place of jealousy. "No, I'm sorry," Morgan said. "It probably isn't my business; I just care about you. You're my friend."

"I appreciate that you care about me," Marina said, dropping back down into the kitchen chair beside Morgan. "I know what I did might seem kind of reckless. But it was something I needed to do." She picked at her short nails. "And that was embarrassing to admit, so it kind of hurt to have my friend—who I trust—judge me for it."

"I'm sorry," Morgan said. "I don't think less of you, you know."

Marina shrugged. "Thanks."

"It's not like I've never slept with somebody… questionable." Morgan gave Marina a smile. "I've never told you about Kelly."

"Kelly from the team?" Marina asked.

Morgan let out a bark of laughter. "Oh, God no. A different Kelly. We met online, but we only went out *once* and basically jumped into bed right away. I don't normally do that. But then again, women don't usually invite themselves back to my house the way she did. I'm used to being in the driver's seat, and it was like she yanked the wheel away. I was too stubborn to admit that it freaked me out to sleep with somebody so fast."

"You slept with her out of stubbornness?" Marina smirked. "That's such a *you* thing to do."

Morgan laughed. "Yeah, well, it was stupid. The sex was terrible. She didn't stop *talking* the entire time; she kept calling me 'baby' and all this stuff even though we'd barely met. It was all so bizarre."

"That sounds awkward," Marina said.

"Yeah. It was super awkward. I didn't call her, and I never heard from her again." Morgan chuckled. "For your sake, I hope your experience was a hell of a lot better."

"It was pretty great, actually." Marina smiled that small, mysterious smile that Morgan loved so much. The thought that she was smiling that way because of another woman caused a prickle of envy that Morgan had to force herself to ignore.

"Yeah? I'm glad." She smiled at her friend. "So, you're definitely a little gay then, huh?"

"More than I knew." Marina grinned back.

"I'm happy for you," Morgan said. It wasn't a lie exactly—she was glad Marina was more secure with herself. But at the same time, it made it even harder to set her own feelings for Marina aside. "So that's that? A one-time thing? Really?"

"That was the plan." Marina rolled her eyes. "Or at least I thought that was the plan."

"What does that mean?" Morgan asked. "Is Jessica wanting to—"

"No, no." Marina shook her head. "It's not her," she said. "Jason's just being a little weird, is all."

"Jealous?" Morgan offered.

"Not so much jealous of Jessica. Maybe he wishes he had been there to watch," Marina said with a bitter little laugh.

Morgan made a sour face. "He really does like the girl-on-girl thing, huh?"

Marina nodded. "It's his favorite fantasy."

"Do you ever worry the reason he's dating you is some sort of bi-girl fetish thing?" Morgan asked.

Marina grimaced. "Well, I do now," she said, scratching her head. "Oh my God, it's going to be so uncomfortable if he ever meets Jessica."

"How would he meet—oh, softball. Do you think he'd recognize her?"

"Yeah." Marina sighed. "But hopefully, I can keep him from *saying* anything to her."

"If it does come out that you two hooked up, do you think it's going to be awkward with the team?" Morgan asked.

"I don't see how it can get much more awkward than it was last game. That was painful," Marina said, shaking her head.

"It really was," Morgan agreed.

"But it'll get better," Marina said as if trying to convince herself. "Jessica wouldn't say anything. And if it did come out, well, I guess telling you was kind of a practice run at explaining it to other people. I'll be less of a mess if it comes up again."

"You weren't a mess," Morgan assured her. "It's a hard thing to talk about."

"You're not wrong. But just because I feel a little more prepared for questions doesn't mean I want to face them—if given a choice." Marina looked at her. "You're not going to tell anybody, are you?"

Morgan put up her hands. "No, of course." She snorted. "Who would I even tell? Things have been awkward with Kelly lately… After that last game, I wasn't sure why I'm on the team at all. I still suck, and I don't really have any friends there."

Marina looked at her with that sweet little smile. "Yes, you do. You've got me. And I hope that no matter what happens with the rest of the team, we'll still be friends."

Morgan's heart skipped a beat. The way Marina was looking at her, her big brown eyes locked on Morgan's face, made the moment feel so intimate. "Of course," Morgan replied, a little breathlessly. "We'll always be friends."

Chapter 14
Marina

Marina's conversation with Morgan about Jessica had been unexpected and difficult but surprisingly cathartic. She'd told Morgan some things that she'd never said out loud before. And it was good to have somebody to talk to about Jessica with. Somebody who *wasn't* going to try to use it to get her into a threesome. Jason was acting insufferable, and it was really wearing on Marina's nerves. *He'll drop it eventually*, she tried to reassure herself. *The idea is just fresh in his mind. He can't obsess about something that's never going to happen indefinitely. He didn't use to be this obsessed.* If Morgan's supposition had been correct—that he was only into her because of some fetish for bi women—it would have come up before now. *Right?*

When Marina got home from Morgan's, she wasn't surprised to find Matt and Evan in the living room watching the game and having beers with Jason. What did surprise her was the standing ovation the two gave her when she came into the room.

"Woo-hoo! Yeah, Marina!" Matt cheered.

"Way to go!" Evan added, clapping loudly.

Marina looked from one to the other and then at her boyfriend, sitting on the sofa, smirking. "Did you *tell* them?" Marina growled.

"I was proud of you, mama," he said. "Gettin' it on with that hottie."

"Yeah, she is *smokin'*," Matt agreed. "I bet it was so hot."

Marina goggled at him. "How do you know what she looks like?"

Jason waved his phone. "We internet stalked her. I'd seen her at your games before, but hot damn!" He handed her the phone, and Marina scrolled through the pictures. Jessica had several scantily clad shots of herself posted on Instagram.

"Did you see that one of her in the little blue bikini?" Evan asked. "I can't believe you hit that. Man, what I would pay to see that."

Marina's head shot up. "Get out!" she snapped. "I mean it. Leave. Now."

"Oh, come on, mama. Chill out; they're only saying good things," Jason said lazily.

She tossed Jason's phone back at him with force. "I don't want to hear them say *anything*!" she shouted. "You had no right to tell them."

"Can you really blame him?" Evan began. "It's just so hot—"

"Fuck off, Evan," Marina cut him off. "I said I don't want to hear it. Now get the hell out of my house. All of you."

Matt and Evan looked at each other and, with a shrug, started to head for the door. "You too," Marina growled at Jason. Matt and Evan froze.

Jason stared blankly at her, uncomprehending. "What?"

"You heard me. Get the fuck out of *my* house." Marina felt so hurt, so betrayed. He'd shared something so deeply personal to her with his buddies just so they could all get off on the idea. It was humiliating. The longer it took Jason to react, the angrier Marina got. "Get off the damn sofa, Jason."

"Fine," Jason rose unsteadily to his feet. "I didn't expect you to be such a bitch about—"

"Fuck off, Jason. Seriously. We're done."

That got his attention. "What?" He starred at her, incredulous. "Just because I told my friends about this one thing, you're seriously breaking up with me?"

"This one thing? Goddamn it, Jason! This was a big deal to me!" Marina heard her voice crack. She looked at Jason, tears filling her eyes. "When you said I could, could be with her, just the one time, I thought you were doing it because you cared about *me*. I thought you cared about how I was feeling about myself. But all you care about is what's in it for you! That it was *hot*. It just was something you could fantasize about and brag about to your friends. Do you know how gross that is? Ugh! And you really thought I was going to have a *threesome* with you, didn't you?"

"Well, yeah, but—"

"Then this is the last straw."

"The last straw? This is one little thing."

"It's not one little thing. It's a hundred little things." She folded her arms. "You don't help me or care for me. You don't respect me. And I'm over it. We're done. Now get out."

There was a stretch of silence. Jason didn't even argue; he just glared at her until Evan put an arm around him and led him to the door. "Come on, man. Let's just give her some space," he said.

"Yeah, man, she'll come around," Matt added as they disappeared through the door.

"No, I won't!" Marina yelled after them. When they were gone, she locked all the doors before she sank to the floor of the kitchen and cried. Scout, who would hide when he heard shouting, came out of the bedroom and nuzzled her face. "Aw, come here," she whispered, tears spilling down her cheeks as it dawned on her that saying goodbye to Jason would mean saying goodbye to his dog as well.

Scout curled up next to her with his head in her lap. "I'm going to miss you, buddy," she whispered. Marina knew detangling her life from Jason's would be more complicated than just kicking him out. But when she realized that she would miss the dog more than her boyfriend, she knew beyond a doubt that breaking up with him was the right thing to do. They'd been together for so long, but had he ever done anything to show that he took the relationship seriously? *If he really loved me, if he was really in this for the long term, why hasn't he made any commitment to me? Why didn't he propose? If this was going to be forever, why is this still* my *house and not* our *house?* Marina wondered if her unconscious mind had known this wouldn't last. Why else hadn't she pushed for those things? *This is for the best.* That didn't mean it didn't hurt, but she went to bed feeling more relief than grief.

Marina woke up the next day expecting to be bombarded by text messages from Jason begging her to take him back, but the texts never came. She didn't want to initiate a conversation, but she did send one text, just to reconfirm to him that she had loved him but that she still wanted to break up. She didn't hear a word back.

Marina went to work, numbed by the monotony of a typical day in the office. At noon her cell rang. "Matt?" Marina answered, ducking out of the bank and walking around the corner.

"Hey, is it okay if I bring the truck over tonight and help Jason get his dog and stuff?" Matt asked. The shock stopped her dead in her tracks. *All that time and this is it? I say we're done, and that's it?* If this was so easy for him, that was just another sign that she'd done the right thing.

"Marina?" Matt's voice came over the phone, bringing Marina back to the present.

"Oh, uh, sure, yeah, that would be fine," she agreed.

"And it would probably be best if you weren't there," Matt said.

"Fine," Marina agreed. "But just tell him he'd better not take anything he didn't pay for himself. That includes the TV."

"Fine," he huffed. "There's no reason for you to be bitch about it. You told him to go, and he's going. He's not exactly happy about this, you know."

She didn't know. How could she know when he hadn't said anything? "Just tell him… tell him I'm sorry it worked out like this, but if he'd just have—"

"Look, I'm going to save you the trouble. I'm not telling him shit for you. We always suspected you were a closet lesbian, but you didn't have to do him like that," Matt growled.

"Closet lesbian? I'm not a lesbian; that's not why I broke up with him!" Marina said, causing a couple in the parking lot to turn and stare. She turned away. "I'm not a lesbian," she repeated.

"Whatever. Just leave my friend alone, alright?" Matt said contemptuously.

"No problem," Marina snapped back and hung up. The whole conversation was so surreal. *Does he really think I'm a lesbian? Is that why he's not fighting me on the breakup?* In a way, it made things easier, but it also made her angry. Sleeping with Jessica didn't make her a lesbian any more than sleeping with him had made her straight.

This is an opportunity to explore that side of myself, Marina realized all at once. She wasn't a lesbian—of this she was certain. But she'd spent so many years exclusively dating men, maybe it was time to turn the tables and date women for a while.

Visions of her romp with Jessica floated through her mind, but Jessica wasn't exactly "girlfriend material." *Morgan is.* Marina shook her head against the intrusive thought. *No, we're just friends. It's not worth risking that.* Even if it were to be a possibility someday, it was far too soon after her breakup with Jason. *I probably shouldn't date anybody for a while. I don't know how to go about dating chicks anyway.* She sighed deeply.

Would it be weird if I asked Morgan for advice? Could she talk to her friend about dating without thinking of her as a potential partner? *It never hurts to try.* If she wasn't going to be home this evening, she would need something to do anyway.

Marina texted Morgan, "Hey, are you up for hanging out tonight?" Morgan didn't reply right away.

She never did during the workday. An hour later, Marina's phone buzzed.

"I was planning on laying the last of the decking tonight, but if you're up for a little physical labor you're more than welcome to join me," Morgan replied, adding, "I can pay you in food."

Marina was surprised; Morgan had never asked her to help with a home renovation project. In fact, she'd gotten the impression that Morgan didn't trust her to perform to her exacting standards. It was flattering that Morgan would ask, besides which Marina wasn't exactly in a position to say no—she had nowhere else to be. "I look forward to it!"

Marina left for Morgan's house with no intention of telling her about the break-up. It had all happened so suddenly; she was still processing it herself and wasn't sure she was ready to talk about it.

Morgan was in the backyard when Marina arrived. She was dressed in paint-covered overalls with nothing but a sports bra beneath them. Her hair was pulled up into a messy bun—something Marina had never seen on her before—and her face was red and glistening with sweat, a smudge of dirt on one cheek. There was something inexplicably sexy about her disheveled look and intense concentration. Morgan didn't notice Marina right away—her focus fully taken by the task of carefully cutting a long deck board. Marina watched her until she was done and had turned off the saw.

"Hey, you started without me," Marina called, stepping closer.

Morgan looked up, and a wide grin spread across her perfect face. "You made it!"

It made Marina's chest warm to see somebody so genuinely happy to see her. It reminded her how long it had been since Jason had looked at her like that. Lately, the only time he seemed excited to see was when he thought he might get laid. *I really did make the right decision.*

Marina smiled back. "I wouldn't have missed it. Morgan VanDolen letting little old me help with a house project? I thought the day would never come."

Morgan laughed out loud. "Don't get too excited. I'm a pretty harsh task-master; you might regret offering to help."

"Bring it on," Marina replied.

"Oh, I will. And who knows, if you pass muster, I might even let you help me in the bedroom." She winked at Marina, and Marina felt her heart skip a beat.

She knew Morgan was teasing and that "help in the bedroom" meant ripping up carpets and repainting walls. Still, for a split second, Marina's mind went to *other* bedroom activities. The thought sent an unexpected bolt of electricity shooting through her body.

"Are you okay?" Morgan asked.

"I broke up with Jason," Marina blurted out.

Morgan blinked at her, her mouth open in unmasked surprise. "What? When?" she asked.

"Just yesterday," said Marina, twisting one of her curls with a finger and averting her eyes from Morgan's intense stare. "That's actually why I asked to come over. Jason and his buddies are moving him out tonight."

"Oh shit, that was quick," Morgan said.

"Yeah. Really, really quick." Marina swallowed hard and recounted the story. By the end, she was near tears. "I know I broke up with him but… but he didn't even… he just… that was it." She lost control and began to cry. *This is why I shouldn't have told her. Morgan doesn't want to see me crying over Jason.* "I'm sorry, it's not your problem, I shouldn't—"

"Shh," Morgan took a step forward and put her arms around Marina. "It's okay. I'm sorry you're going through this," she whispered.

"Thanks," Marina leaned into her. Morgan smelled of sawdust and faint perfume. And her embrace was comforting, like being wrapped in a warm blanket on a cold winter day. "You're a good friend," she said.

"I try," Morgan replied.

Reluctantly, Marina stepped out of the embrace. She looked around. "So, should we get to work on this deck or what?"

"Ever used a nail gun before?" Morgan asked. Marina shook her head. "Don't worry. It's easy; I'll show you."

It wasn't nearly as easy as Morgan made it look. It was heavy and jumped against the wood scraps Morgan had rightfully insisted she practice on. Morgan offered to give her another job, but Marina was stubborn. With focused determination, she conquered the task, and Morgan let her graduate to nailing in the actual decking.

They got into a rhythm, and time slipped easily by. The sun dipped below the treetops just as they laid the last few boards.

"I think that does it," Morgan said, wiping sweat from her brow and looking up at the darkening sky. "And just in time too. It's great that we got it done so quickly. I thought for sure it would be a two-day process."

"It would have been, without my *fantastic* help," Marina teased.

Morgan laughed. "You're not wrong. Thank you. Really."

"Thank you for giving me something to do today." Marina hopped up to sit on the newly completed deck. It wasn't far off the grass—tall enough to feel elevated but without being so far off the ground to require a guard rail. She kicked her feet, dangling over the edge, and stretched her arms. "It was a good workout," she said. Her muscles tingled and twitched from so much time with the powerful nail gun. "I'm going to be sore tomorrow."

"That's what she said!" Morgan smirked at her.

"I've been a bad influence on you," Marina said with a laugh.

"Perhaps." Morgan looked sideways at her and winked. "But I like it."

They sat quietly for a moment, looking out on the lawn scattered with tools and the remnants of wood. It was peaceful. The fireflies were out, their little bursts of light like tiny fireworks sporadically erupting here and there across the backyard.

"I believe I owe you dinner," Morgan said, breaking the silence. "We just have to clean up; I can't go back inside until the tools are packed away, and the scrap wood is," she gestured vaguely at the lawn, "not like this. I'm a bit of a stickler. Sorry."

"No problem," Marina said, hopping off the deck.

"I'll turn on the back lights," Morgan said.

Marina watched her reach inside the sliding glass door. When the floodlights blinked on, the sudden brightness nearly blinded her. She turned away from the lights to the yard, blinking against the spots in her vision. The bright bulbs had illuminated the yard like police searchlights, casting long shadows across the grass.

Still blinking, Marina began to wander the yard, picking up bits of discarded lumber. Between the dark shadows and the spots in her eyes, she didn't see the saw until it was too late. She tripped, and when she hit the ground, searing pain shot through her leg, just above her knee. Marina screamed. She rolled over and grabbed her leg. She could feel the slickness of blood under her hand. Fear and pain made her breath come out in gasps.

Morgan was at Marina's side in a flash. "What happened?"

"The saw," Marina said through gritted teeth. "I didn't see it." She sucked in a breath. "But I felt it." She was too scared to cry—she could hardly breathe. Shaking, she moved her hand to show Morgan the gash; she didn't look at it herself. She couldn't.

Morgan's expression was unreadable. "Keep pressure on it," she said, putting Marina's hand back in place over the wound.

"Okay."

Before Marina knew what was happening, Morgan scooped her up into her arms and began carrying her across the lawn. "What are you doing?" she asked, her voice breathless. She was getting light-headed. *How much blood am I losing?* Marina wasn't good with blood; she started to worry she might pass out.

"I'm taking you inside," Morgan grunted as she stepped up onto the deck, still carrying Marina.

"Shouldn't I go to a doctor?" Marina asked, trying not to panic.

"I *am* a doctor," Morgan said firmly, yanking open the door and stepping into the warm lights of the kitchen.

"But you're a dermatologist," Marina said. Fear was starting to get the better of her.

"A dermatologist *is* a doctor." Morgan set her down gently on a kitchen chair, Marina's hand still gripping her thigh. Morgan gingerly lifted Marina's hand and looked at the wound. Marina stole a glance down at her leg and immediately wished she hadn't. Blood was everywhere. When she caught a glimpse of the inside of her leg, she turned her head and vomited on the beautiful wood floor.

"I'm sorry," she croaked.

"Don't be. That's a perfectly normal reaction." Morgan put a towel over the wound, and Marina writhed in pain. Morgan put Marina's hand back into place. "Keep up the pressure. Try to stay calm. I'll be right back."

"Please don't leave," Marina begged in a childlike whine that she usually would have been embarrassed about, but it just hurt so damn bad. She was past pride.

Morgan crouched so that she was nose to nose with Marina. "Look at me," she said. "You're going to be okay. I'm just going upstairs to get some things out of my medicine cabinet." Her eyes searched Marina's face. "Do you trust me?"

Marina nodded.

"Good. Don't move; I'll be as quick as I can." Morgan stood and walked off toward the stairs.

In the silent kitchen, the sound of her heartbeat thundered in Marina's ears, beating out a rhythm of fear and trepidation. *Morgan knows what she's doing,* Marina tried to calm herself, but her chest still felt tight, like she was fighting for breath. She squeezed her eyes shut. "Morgan knows what she's doing," she whispered to herself.

"Yes, I do. And you're going to be alright." Morgan's voice was calm and it soothed Marina to have her back at her side. "Now lay back and try to remember to breathe. This is going to sting."

"What are you going to do?" Marina added, her body already tense in anticipation of more pain.

"I'm going to clean out the wound. That's going to be the worst part. Then I am going to use superglue to close the wound."

"Superglue?!" Marina repeated, horrified. "Are you sure you're a doctor?"

Morgan actually laughed. "Yes, I went to medical school. I could use something called liquid stitches, but this does the same thing and stings a hell of a lot less."

"But… it'll work?" Marina asked in a squeak.

"Yes." She stopped and looked at Marina. "But if you don't want me to do it, I won't. We could go to an ER, and they might choose traditional stitches, but I think that this will be just as effective and faster. And I can do it right now. Would you like to go to the ER?"

"No," Marina took a deep breath and shook her head. "I trust you."

Morgan nodded once and got back to work, her lips pressed tight in concentration. She had been right; cleaning it hurt even worse than the initial cut, and Marina had to grit her teeth to keep from screaming. She believed Morgan when she said it wasn't serious, but at the same time, she felt as if somebody had attempted to amputate her leg.

"You're doing great," Morgan cooed as she worked. "Now, I'm going to put on some ointment before I close it up."

Marina nodded but didn't say anything; she couldn't have formed coherent words if she'd wanted to. The pain was hot, as if she were being welded back together with a flaming torch—the ointment like molten metal oozing into her leg.

Marina let out a sharp gasp when Morgan pulled the skin together to apply the glue. She clenched her jaw and tried to focus on breathing as Morgan finished closing the wound. The sensation had gone beyond pain now and become surreal. Feeling Morgan pull and prod at her leg was like an out-of-body experience.

"All done, for now," Morgan said, leaning back.

"For now?" Marina asked her chest heaving. She looked down. The blood had been washed away, but the wound was still horrifying to see, and she quickly averted her eyes.

"The glue has to dry," Morgan said. "Then I can put a bandage over it. In the meantime, I can give you some Tylenol." She stood and moved to walk away. Marina reached out grabbed her wrist.

"Don't leave," Marina said, her voice coming out in a squeak. Again, she felt she should be embarrassed, but she didn't have the energy for embarrassment.

Morgan knelt down beside her; she squeezed Marina's hand and looked at her with such tenderness. "You're probably going to feel a bit of a crash now. How about I move you to the sofa?"

Marina nodded and Morgan scooped her up into her arms again as if she weighed nothing. Marina winced as Morgan bent to lay her down gently onto the sofa. She could feel her leg throb with pain but relaxing into the soft cushions gave her some measure of relief.

"I am going to have to leave you for a minute now and get that Tylenol," Morgan said after she'd slipped her arms out from under Marina. "As the initial shock wears off, it's going to hurt more. Tylenol isn't perfect, but it'll take the edge off." Morgan touched Marina's face, brushing away the curls that stuck to her sweaty forehead and tucking them behind her ear. The motion was so intimate.

Marina looked into Morgan's memorizing blue eyes. "Morgan…" she began.

"I'll be right back." Morgan squeezed her hand once more and left the room. Marina laid back against the sofa pillows and closed her eyes. She was suddenly so tired.

Chapter 15
Morgan

Morgan felt horrible about what had happened to Marina. Although she appeared outwardly calm, Morgan's heart hammered angrily against her ribcage. Stepping away to retrieve a Tylenol gave her the chance to breathe and try to get her pulse under control. She wiped a hand across her face. *Get it together. She's going to be okay. Just take care of her.*

When Morgan returned with the pain reliever, Marina's eyes were closed. "Marina?" she called softly, but Marina didn't stir. *She's asleep.* It was no wonder; her body had been through a rollercoaster of pain and shock. Morgan watched Marina sleep, her arms crossed on her chest like Snow White, her dark hair contrasting her pale skin. Color was slowly returning to her face, and her breathing had grown steadier. Morgan set the Tylenol and a glass of water beside the couch, within

Marina's reach, but she didn't wake her. *She must be so exhausted.*

After assuring herself that Marina would be okay on her own, Morgan went into the kitchen to clean up the floor where Marina had gotten sick. Once that was taken care of, she went upstairs to shower and change. Her clothing was covered in dirt, sawdust, and Marina's blood. As the shower warmed up, she looked at the bloodstains on her overalls. The heart-pounding adrenalin was draining away, and guilt had begun to gnaw at her insides. *I should have been more responsible.*

Morgan set the pants in the sink to soak and stepped into the shower. *The deck is my project; those were my tools. Marina getting hurt is my fault.* On a day when Marina was already hurting emotionally, Morgan had gotten her physically injured as well. *What the hell, VanDolen?* She knew that if she had been working on the deck alone, she would have stopped before dark, her things would have been in better order, and there wouldn't have been random lumbar and tools lying around the yard. *I shouldn't have asked her to help me.*

Morgan washed quickly and stepped back out of the shower wrapped in a towel. She glanced once more at the blood-stained overalls. *There's no point in dwelling on it.* What had happened had happened. It was over and done with. Morgan would learn from it, move on, and do better in the future.

Dressed in comfortable sweatpants and a t-shirt, Morgan crept downstairs. If Marina was still asleep, she didn't want to wake her. But when she reached the landing, she saw that Marina was sitting up on the couch, sipping the water Morgan had left for her.

"You're awake," Morgan said, stating the obvious. "Did you take the Tylenol?"

Marina nodded. "Yeah, thanks. Although I don't know that it's agreeing with my stomach. I think I need to eat something."

Food, of course. Morgan mentally smacked herself for not ordering before she showered. "I'll get food ordered right away. We were going to do pizza, right?" Morgan asked.

"I can order it if you'd hand me my phone. I am the one who invited herself over after all—"

"Forget it. You helped me build my deck and were rewarded with a near-maiming. Pizza is the *least* I can do," Morgan insisted, picking up her phone.

"I got hurt because I wasn't paying attention, and you're also the one who fixed me up," Marina countered. "I owe *you* one."

Morgan shook her head. "I'm ordering pizza, and that's final. And until it gets here, I can bring you snacks or anything else you need." She crouched down beside the couch. "I am so, so sorry this happened, Marina."

"Please don't be; it's not your fault." Marina reached out and squeezed Morgan's shoulder. "Really. Don't beat yourself up over it."

"Alright. But if there's anything I can do, just name it."

"Actually," Marina said, brushing a lock of Morgan's wet hair from her shoulder. "Could you help me get cleaned up? I feel so gross, but I probably can't just hop in a shower." She looked at her leg. "So to speak.

Morgan wasn't expecting that. *Help Marina shower?* The idea made her knees weak and her chest tight. Morgan gave Marina a stiff, business-like nod, trying to hide her emotions behind her practiced physician's exterior. "Come on, I can get you set up in the shower in a way that will work."

Marina winced and sucked in air between her teeth when Morgan helped her off the sofa. In response, Morgan moved to pick her up again, but Marina waved her off. "I can do it; I just need a little help."

Instead of carrying her, Morgan put her arm around Marina's waist and helped her hobble over the bathroom.

The shower, which Morgan had so painstakingly tiled herself, wasn't going to be safe for Marina hopping around on one foot. The clean, modern design didn't have a ledge to sit on or handholds to steady oneself. Luckily, Morgan had a small folding shower seat that she had bought while doing the tiling to save her back during some of the more awkward wall sections. She unfolded it and helped Marina into it.

"Thank you so much, I think a shower is going to feel so good," Marina said, crossing her arms and pulling her shirt up and over her head. "Do you think you could help me get it started? Is it okay for the glue to get wet?" Marina asked as Morgan stood, awestruck—frozen like a deer in headlights—as Marina began to undress in front of her without the slightest hesitation.

Morgan quickly averted her eyes but not before she'd gotten an eyeful of Marina's perfect little breasts and light brown nipples. Morgan felt her cheeks warm and heat build within her, but she tried to cool her attraction. Morgan was a doctor, and today Marina wasn't a pretty woman she had a crush on; she was a patient.

"Yes and no," Morgan said, getting ahold of herself. "It's okay if it gets a little wet, but you don't want it directly in the water. Here, let me warm up the shower, and once you're settled, I can point the showerhead at your back." Morgan turned her back to Marina and began to fuss with the shower handle, hyperaware of Marina's state of undress and the effect it was having on her.

"Thank you so much," Marina said. "I'm sorry I said that thing about you just being a dermatologist. I'm really lucky you're a doctor."

"Don't even worry about it," Morgan said, testing the water temperature with her hand. Once it was warm enough, she turned back around. Marina had removed her shorts and was just easing her panties down and off over her injured leg, careful not to let them touch the wounded area. Morgan watched her; the hot blood coursing through her seemed to be flowing away from her head and concentrating somewhere else entirely. She kept her eyes glued to Marina's injury as Marina tossed her last item of clothing from the shower.

"Morgan?" Marina looked up at her.

"I have the water ready," Morgan said a little too quickly, her eyes darting up to meet Marina's. "Just let me know when you're ready, and I'll move the… the thing." She gestured at the showerhead. Marina smiled that small, alluring smile.

"I'm ready," she said, and Morgan diverted the water until the stream rained down on Marina's back and shoulders.

"How's that?" Morgan asked.

"It feels great. Thank you," Marina said, closing her eyes and leaning back into the spray until the water ran over her face, down her neck to her chest. Morgan swallowed *hard*. She had already thought that Marina was just about the most beautiful woman she'd ever seen. With her eyes closed, head back, dripping wet, Marina wasn't merely beautiful; she was the most panty-soaking, mouthwateringly *sexy* woman on the planet.

The desire to touch her was palpable, almost irresistible; Morgan had to turn away. "I'll leave you to it, then. There's soap over by your shoulder—"

"Wait, Morgan?" Marina called to her.

"Yes?" Morgan asked, turning back.

"Would you help me wash my legs? I'm can't really lean over well, but there's still some blood and…" Marina looked down. "I don't do well with blood."

"Oh, yeah, sure. No problem." Morgan took the washcloth from Marina's outstretched hand. Her heart skipped a beat as she knelt down, just outside the lip of the shower. Marina was sitting on the shower seat, her legs crossed, the injured leg on top. Conscious to not let her eyes wander higher than the wound, Morgan gently cleaned Marina's lower leg from her knees to her feet. Morgan felt like a devotee, washing the feet of her Goddess. By the time she was done, her clothes were soaked from errant spray.

"I should go change," Morgan said, standing. "I'll bring you something to wear for when you're done. Just give me a shout if you need help with anything else."

"Thanks again, Morgan," Marina said. "You're the best friend in the world."

Morgan smiled at her. "No problem." She winked. "It's what I do."

When Morgan closed the bathroom door behind herself, she put her hand over her heart, let out a sigh, and leaned back against the door. *Oh my God. Get a hold of yourself, VanDolen.* Her heart was pounding again, but not from fear—from attraction. Her t-shirt and sweats weren't the only wet items of clothing she would need to change when she went upstairs. Being in the room with Marina, naked and wet; caressing her smooth calf as she washed her; the whole situation had unleashed a monsoon in her panties.

After a few deep breaths, Morgan got ahold of herself and trudged up the stairs to change and hunt down some clothes that would work for petite little Marina. When she returned downstairs, she could hear that the shower had been turned off. She knocked on the door. "Marina? I've got clothes for you? Do you need—"

"Come on in," Marina called from inside the door. Morgan braced herself for another teasingly fantastic view of Marina naked as she turned the knob. Marina was seated on the stool, wrapped in the soft gray towel

Morgan had left for her. Morgan felt both relief and disappointment and prayed neither showed.

"I brought you some things. They might be a tad big, but the sweatpants have a drawstring. Oh, and I thought maybe borrowing girl underwear might be a bit... awkward, but I figured boxers might be okay? I hope that's alright." Morgan handed her the stack of neatly folded clothing.

"Thank you." Marina quickly slid the towel down and slipped on the t-shirt giving Morgan another brief unintended glimpse of her perfect breasts. Morgan started to back away, but Marina grabbed her arm. "Help me stand?" she asked. "I worry about slipping."

"Of course." Morgan held Marina steady as she stood and gingerly stepped into the boxers. She winced when she put her weight on the injured leg to lift the other. "Ooh, that hurts." She quickly slipped her foot in so that she could shift her weight back to the uninjured side. "Would it be okay if I skip the sweatpants? I think I think they might rub on it."

"Oh, of course." Morgan shook her head. "I don't know what I was thinking."

The doorbell rang just as Morgan was easing Marina down onto the couch. "That'll be the pizza." She went to the door to retrieve their dinner. After grabbing a couple of plates from the kitchen, Morgan sat down beside Marina.

Marina smiled when Morgan handed her a plateful of pizza. "Thank you," she said. She laughed. "I feel like I've said that a hundred times, but really, really. Thank you."

"Of course. Pizza had been part of the deal to begin with. Everything else was just a bonus," Morgan grinned. "And when we're done eating, I can give you a ride home. No charge," she teased.

"Actually, I was hoping…" Marina chewed her lip a moment before asking, "can I stay here tonight?"

You can stay here forever, Morgan thought. Marina's looked so damn pretty right out of the shower, with her wet hair and flushed cheeks. And she was so adorable how she kept thanking her and even when the accident was Morgan's fault in the first place. Marina was amazing. Morgan would never kick Marina out, not in a million years.

"Yes, of course you can stay," Morgan said, trying to sound casual rather than like the smitten melty mess she felt like on the inside. "Mi casa es su casa."

"Thanks," Marina said. She looked at Morgan with her big brown eyes and Mona Lisa smile. "Actually," she added, setting down her plate. "I have one more thing I'd like to ask…"

"Sure, anything. You name it," Morgan replied.

"Would… would you kiss me?"

Morgan's heart stopped dead in her chest. "Are you sure?" she asked, her voice coming out in a breathy whisper. Marina nodded, her eyes searching Morgan's face, her expression somewhere between longing and fear. Morgan put a hand on her cheek. It was so warm in her palm. She leaned her head forward, and their lips met. The kiss was tentative at first. Part of Morgan couldn't believe this was truly what Marina wanted, but Marina leaned into the kiss, her lips parting slightly, her hand coming around to the back of Morgan's neck, pulling her in deeper. It was quite possibly the best kiss of Morgan's life.

After a moment, Marina pulled back to look at her. "I really like you, Morgan."

"I really like you too," Morgan replied. Marina smiled and moved to kiss her again. Morgan pulled her onto her lap, careful not to bump Marina's injured leg. Marina reacted by wrapping her arms around Morgan's neck and kissing her fiercely. Morgan's toes tingled as they kissed again and again. They kissed until the pizza had grown cold, and Morgan's leg had gone numb from the weight of Marina on her lap.

"So, does this mean we're dating now?" Marina asked when they came up for air.

"Are you ready for that?" Morgan asked. "I know you *just* broke up with—"

"Yes," Marina said quickly. "Absolutely."

"And Jessica?"

Marina slid off her lap, and Morgan worried that she was angry. *I shouldn't have mentioned Jessica.*

"Morgan, do you know why I picked Jessica to sleep with, even though I am much more attracted to you?" she asked.

"You are?" Morgan's chest warmed with pleasure.

"Yes, of course." Marina shook her head. "But I knew that if I slept with you, it could never have been just sex. I like you too much. I would have… I just knew if I slept with you there would be a good chance that I would fall in love with you. And I wasn't ready to take that risk."

Morgan hadn't thought her heart could beat any harder but when Marina said the word "love," her cardiac rhythm went into overdrive, fluttering as rapidly as a hummingbird's wings. "But you're ready now?" Morgan asked. Marina nodded. "What changed?"

"I let Jason go," Marina said. "I realized that I was holding on to something that wasn't going anywhere. And I realized that… that I was spending more time thinking about you than I ever had thought about anybody before. Meeting you jumpstarted all these feelings I that I never thought I…" She shook her head like she couldn't find quite the right words. She put a hand on Morgan's cheek. "I think this could really go somewhere. And I'd risk anything to give that a chance."

Morgan leaned forward and kissed her. After a few passionate, wonderful, exciting kisses, Marina pulled away. "What about you?" she asked. "Do you think this could really be something real?"

"Absolutely," Morgan quickly affirmed. "The second I saw you, I wanted you. And once I got to know you, I knew I wanted to be *with* you—even if I could only ever be your friend. You're an incredible person, and I'd be the luckiest girl alive if you would be my girlfriend."

"It's settled then." Marina pulled her in and kissed her.

This is real. We're really going to do this. Morgan didn't know she'd ever been happier in her life.

.

Chapter 16
Marina

Marina rolled over and was jolted awake by the pain in her leg. It was dark in Morgan's bedroom. Marina looked at her phone. *Barely after five AM.* She sighed and tried to get comfortable without waking Morgan. Her leg throbbed. The Tylenol Morgan had given her when they'd gone to bed must have worn off. Marina rolled to her back. *I'm not getting back to sleep, am I?* She looked to her right, where Morgan lay sleeping. Her teammate-turned-girlfriend was breathing steadily, her chest moving up and down, a small audible huff of air coming out with each exhale.

Marina was still in awe of the whole situation. When she'd asked Morgan if she could come over yesterday, she never would have guessed that it could end like this: in bed together with her new girlfriend. They hadn't had sex last night, only kissed and cuddled—careful not to bump her wounded leg. In a way—several ways really—Marina was grateful for her accident last night.

If Morgan hadn't needed to care for her so intimately, they probably wouldn't have ended up making out on the sofa. The night would have ended like all her other nights with Morgan: pizza, laughter, and a wave goodnight before walking home alone. She would take a goodnight kiss over a goodbye wave any day. And the way that Morgan had tended to her—Marina had never felt so cared for in her life.

A warm feeling filled Marina's heart when she thought of all Morgan had done for her. She smiled when she recalled the look on Morgan's face when she'd undressed for the shower, her cheeks flushing pink, her eyes darting around like she was trying to look at anything but her bare chest. Marina wasn't trying to be provocative. She just wasn't a particularly modest person. And given that Morgan was acting as her doctor, Marina had almost forgotten about her crush. Morgan's reaction was an adorable reminder of her attraction.

But the care Morgan had shown while tending to her told Marina her feelings went deeper than physical attraction. Morgan *liked* her—really liked her. And that thought filled Marina with joy. And now here she was, lying in bed beside her. It was like a dream come true.

However, Marina's body wasn't going to let her lay there much longer. *Stupid bladder.* As quietly as possible, Marina pulled back the covers and sat up on the side of the bed. She put her good foot down first and stood up. Gingerly she tested out her injured leg. The pain tore through her leg as if the wound itself was ripping open. She gasped and lifted the foot back up off the floor. *Well shit.* Using a hand on the bed to help steady herself, Marina started to hop toward the bathroom.

"What are you doing? Let me help you." Morgan was out of bed and at her side before Marina even knew she'd woken up.

"It's okay, you didn't have to—" Marina began.

"Oh, shut up and let me help you or I'll pick you up and carry you again," Morgan said with a snort of laughter.

"Okay, okay," Marina acquiesced, putting her arm around Morgan. "That was very impressive, by the way. You're really strong."

"I know," Morgan said, winking at her.

Marina laughed out loud. When they reached the door to the bathroom, Marina retracted her arm. "I think

I can get it from here," she said. She went up onto her tiptoe and kissed Morgan on the cheek. "Thank you."

Morgan tilted her chin up and kissed her lightly on the lips. "Any time, beautiful."

Marina shook her head. She hobbled to the bathroom and shut the door. When she finished, Morgan was waiting with Tylenol and water in hand. Marina took the pills and let Morgan help her back into bed. She cuddled up to Morgan. "This is really nice," she said sleepily.

"It really is."

It was the first in a series of nice days waking up in Morgan's bed and of being cared for by her new girlfriend. Morgan was Marina's first real girlfriend, and she was an exceptional one. She tended to her medically—providing Marina with crutches and medications—she shuttled her back and forth from her house when she needed things; she even drove her to work.

The worst part of being "slightly maimed"—as Morgan put it—was that she wouldn't be able to play softball for a few weeks. But that didn't mean that she couldn't watch and cheer on her team. Marina had texted the Dirt Bunnies about her injury in advance, but she hadn't told them about her new relationship with Morgan.

The two of them rolled into the parking lot for the next game together in Morgan's jeep. Marina hopped out and hobbled over to the diamond while Morgan grabbed her gear from the back. The team immediately descended upon Marina, surrounding her, and expressing sympathy and curiosity at the state of her injury.

"How did you manage to get yourself in the leg like that?" Liz asked.

"I basically tripped and fell onto the saw in the dark," Marina replied, wincing at the memory.

"That was my fault," Morgan said, joining the group. "She was helping me with my deck project, and I waited too long to start wrapping things up for the night."

"You let somebody help you with something?" Kelly asked, raising an eyebrow at Morgan.

Morgan grinned. "Marina's good at helping me with all sorts of things." She caught Marina's eye and winked. Marina still melted a little inside every time Morgan did that.

"You've been helping me more," Marina replied. "I'm basically living with you."

"Wait, what?" Kelly's eyes went wide.

Shit. Marina had said it without thinking. She and Morgan had agreed not to tell the team they were dating. "Because of my injury," Marina hastened to add. "And because Jason was moving out and—"

"Wait, you broke up with Jason?" Jessica interrupted. She lowered her voice. "Was it because… you know." She gave Marina a significant look. She couldn't say "because we slept together" in front of the team, but Marina knew that's what she was asking.

"Sort of…"

"Because of what?" Kelly asked.

Marina shook her head. "It doesn't matter. There was so much wrong with that relationship. It's good that it's over." Marina felt her cheeks burning under her teammates' intense attention. "Hey, you guys should get out there," she said, nodding toward the diamond. "Good luck!"

"She's right; let's get focused on the game," Morgan added, and the team moved away to start the game.

Jessica lingered. "Hey, I'm sorry if I caused trouble for you," she said.

"Not, it's okay. It's not your fault. There was so much else going on. It was my idea anyway, not yours," Marina insisted. She lowered her voice. "And it was fun. Totally worth it."

Jessica tittered. "Yeah, it was. Well, now that you're free, if you're ever in the mood…" She trailed off suggestively.

"Oh, no, I…" Marina glanced at Morgan, warming up on the field.

Jessica followed her gaze. "Oh, so *that's* a thing now, huh?" She nudged Marina playfully in the ribs.

Marina put her finger to her lips. "Shh. We're not telling people yet."

"Don't worry, I am a picture of discretion." She winked and trotted off to join the rest of the team.

It felt odd to watch and not play. Marina initially seated herself on the bleachers, but sitting made her antsy, and she ended up standing by the dugout, shouting and cheering and doing all she could to feel like a part of the team.

The Dirt Bunnies played a fantastic game, and Morgan was on fire. She had several runs and tagged people out like a pro. The game ended in a decisive victory.

"You played amazing!" Marina gushed to Morgan when the game was over.

"I was thinking about you the whole time," Morgan said with a wide grin. She was beaming with pride. *She's so hot when she's happy.*

Without thinking, Marina reached up and kissed her girlfriend. "Oops," she said, pulling away when she realized what she'd done. She turned to see if anybody had noticed. They had. Liz was staring, open-mouthed. Kelly's eyebrows were raised so high they almost disappeared into her hair. And Jessica was giggling and shaking her head.

Marina turned back to Morgan. "Oh my God, I'm sorry. I know we weren't going to tell people—"

Morgan took Marina's face in her hands, interrupting her with a deep kiss. "It's okay," she said. "Keeping it quiet was your idea, remember?"

"Right." Marina let out a breath. She turned back to the others. *Let the teasing commence.*

"Good for you," Truck said cheerfully.

Not everybody was so positive. Liz pursed her lips and looked the couple up and down. "So, you date one chick, and suddenly you're U-hauling on the first date? That's not how it usually works, you know. We're not all walking clichés," she said acerbically.

"We're not U-hauling," Morgan snapped back.

"I'm going back home tomorrow," Marina blurted out, although she'd never discussed it with Morgan. And based on the look on Morgan's face, she hadn't expected it. A moment of tense silence passed before anybody spoke.

"Well, I think it's great," Jessica piped up. "You two are *too* cute."

Heads nodded, and people moved on to other conversations. Marina and Morgan disengaged with the group and made their way back to Morgan's jeep.

"Are you really been planning on leaving tomorrow?" Morgan asked.

Is it my imagination, or does she look hurt? Marina sighed. "No. I mean, I hadn't planned anything. It just came out."

"Oh."

"It might be the right thing to do though. I can't avoid my house forever. I should, you know, get back to normal." Marina looked at Morgan's face, searching for some indication of what she was thinking. When she didn't say anything, Marina felt compelled to continue. "I really appreciate all that you've done for me. Thank you. Truly."

"Of course. I like taking care of you," Morgan said. "I don't like that you got hurt, but I'm glad I could help. And if you feel like you're ready to go back home, I'll support that too."

"Thanks," Marina said. She wasn't sure she was ready to go home, but Liz's comment had gotten her thinking. Their relationship was brand new. If they wanted it to last, they should give it the space to grow naturally, like a normal relationship, without the complication of Morgan acting as her caregiver. "I think I should go home tomorrow."

Chapter 17

Morgan

It had been an unpleasant surprise when Marina had decided to move back home. The first few days without Marina in her bed were harder than Morgan would have expected. Doubts wiggled their way into her mind. They'd gotten together amid the aftermath of Marina's breakup and sudden physical trauma. Morgan wondered if they would survive as a couple now that Marina no longer needed to be cared for. It felt as if the relationship took a step back when Marina left Morgan's house. They still saw each other frequently. They kissed and cuddled, but a voice in the back of Morgan's mind whispered questions. *Is this going anywhere? Will she ever love me? Or is this some twist on a Florence Nightingale Effect? Once she heals, will we go back to being nothing more than friends?*

Morgan could feel herself falling in love with Marina a little more each day. But the only progression she saw in Marina was with her injury. Marina was healing quickly. In a couple short weeks, she was walking without crutches. And still, Morgan was caught off guard when she started talking about playing softball.

"I want to play in the next Dirt Bunnies game," Marina said out of the blue. She was lying across Morgan's lap in the living room, surrounded by half-eaten containers of Thai food.

"Are you sure you're ready?" Morgan asked, unable to keep the doubt from her voice.

"I think so." Marina looked up at her, regarding Morgan with her dark, thoughtful eyes. "I know it's not perfect, but it's really not *bad* either—just a little sore." She smiled. "I don't even worry that my leg is going to burst open like a bloody piñata anymore."

Morgan smiled back and leaned down to plant a curry-flavored kiss on Marina's lips. "If you say so."

Morgan wanted to trust that Marina knew her own body. But when game day arrived, Morgan found herself filled with anxiety. Anybody could see that Marina still wasn't one hundred percent. There was a hesitancy in the way she moved during warm-ups.

"I'm reassigning Marina to third base," Liz told the team. "Lindsey, take shortstop."

Marina rolled her eyes, but she didn't argue.

"And, Marina, if you ever need to tap out—" Liz began.

"I'll be fine," Marina assured her.

"Okay, let's play some ball." Liz gave Marina a hearty pat on the back. Secretly Morgan wished Liz hadn't let Marina play at all.

Morgan couldn't shake her foreboding feeling as the game got underway. She was distracted—but not in the way Marina normally distracted her. This sort of tense concern didn't help her game. It did the opposite. It caused her to make stupid mistakes, and her mistakes made her frustrated, and the more frustrated she got, the more mistakes she made. Marina was encouraging during the transitions between innings, but Morgan could feel herself getting more and more mired in her own aggravation.

The team they were playing against didn't get a lot of hits, but thanks to the Dirt Bunnies' terrible fielding, they made each connection count. The Dirt Bunnies didn't do much better at batting. Marina got a few good hits, but she just couldn't get on base fast enough.

Morgan could see the disappointment in Marina's posture every time she wasn't fast enough to complete a play, and it killed her. Morgan hated that she couldn't do anything to help her. *She shouldn't have played today. Not that I'm doing any better.*

Morgan's playing was worse than ever. It was like she'd gone back to square one. Morgan's frustration built into anger as the game slowly came to its disappointing but inevitable conclusion: the Dirt Bunnies lost.

"We should have beat this team," Morgan grumbled to herself after the closing handshake. She hated how much of it was her own damn fault. "Fucking hell." Morgan kicked at the wire fencing. She was frustrated; she felt like she was back to being a drain on the team— like all her improvement over the last few months had been nothing more than a fluke. Worse than that, she felt like she'd let Marina down. It was her first game back, and it had been miserable. *Calm your shit, VanDolen.* Morgan had no idea why one stupid softball game was making her so damn angry right now, but it was.

"Morgan." Liz pulled her aside, away from the team as everybody filed off the field. "You need to cut it out and calm the hell down. We didn't win this game, and that's too bad. Nobody likes to lose. But your mood is bringing us down even more than the loss."

"I know," Morgan growled. "I don't want to be this pissed off. But we might not have lost if I—"

"Oh, shut up already!" Liz snapped. "We get it; you think you should be better. But your attitude is far worse than your skills. You think your performance today was shit? Well, your attitude stinks way worse. And I'm sick of it. Either find a new temperament before the next game or don't show up at all. Understood?"

Morgan took a deep breath, straitening to her full height. "Understood," she said, looking down at Liz, her jaw clenched.

Liz let out a little huff. "Good. Now walk away," she said.

"Excuse me?" Morgan blinked at her.

"I can't look at you anymore today. We all just want to enjoy our beer now," Liz said, gesturing over her shoulder to where the team was gathering in the parking lot, most of them trying—and failing—to pretend that they weren't listening to every word Liz was saying. "Do us all a favor and *don't* join us."

"Fine." Morgan turned on her heel and stomped off in the direction of home. It wasn't until she'd arrived at her house that she realized she'd left all her gear *and Marina* back at the park. "Fucking fuck! What is wrong with me?" Morgan fumed, slamming the toe of her shoe into the side of the garage.

"What's with you and kicking things today?" Marina's voice was light and teasing. Morgan turned around. Marina was standing at the bottom of the driveway, her arms full of Morgan's things.

"How did you—?" Morgan began before she saw Kelly, waving from inside her car on the street behind Marina.

"Kelly gave me a ride," Marina said, turning to nod to their teammate. Kelly drove off. "Here, I've got your stuff."

"Thank you," Morgan said. "I'm sorry a stormed off like that. I lost my head a little."

"What's wrong?" Marina added, walking toward Morgan. She still limped a little when she walked, although she swore up and down that she felt fine. Morgan rushed to take the gear from her arms.

"I don't know. I guess I'm in a bad mood. I always hate losing, but... I don't know. Today felt like a step back in my playing. The last couple of games had gone so well." Morgan didn't want to think she'd gone backward. "I haven't been practicing as much—"

"Since I got hurt?" Marina finished. "I'm sorry about that. You had been playing better. Today's on me."

"No, no. This isn't your fault." She sighed. "I'm sorry, I really have my head up my ass today." She lightly touched Marina's face. "I *was* a little nervous about you getting hurt, but I was also really looking forward to having you back out there. I think maybe I put too much pressure on the game because of it. That's on me. Not you." She kissed Marina.

"Are you sure?" Marina asked.

"Positive," Morgan assured her. She wanted to wrap Marina in her arms, but her hands were full of softball gear. "Are you free now?" Morgan asked.

"As a bird," Marina replied.

"Sweet. Let me pack this away, and then we can go inside?"

"Lead the way." Marina gestured forward.

Morgan led Marina to the garage, where she kept her sporting gear during the warmer months. As Morgan put away her softball things, Marina wandered through the garage, over to where Morgan had recently laid out her hockey equipment in preparation for an upcoming tournament. Marina had never seen her hockey equipment before, Morgan realized. She was looking over it with fascination.

"Why do you have so much pink gear?" Marina asked, picking up a glove and studying it. "It doesn't really fit with the rest of your... I don't know... aesthetic?"

"Because of my mom." Morgan surprised herself by answering honestly. She didn't usually talk about her mom. In fact, she actively avoided explaining her gear to most people who asked because it was a painful subject.

"Your mom?" Marina echoed.

Morgan took a deep breath. She was generally content to let people think she was just some weirdo who needed to stand out as much as possible. She knew it was part of the reason half the hockey league hated her, and she didn't care. But Marina wasn't just anybody. "Yeah, she was diagnosed with breast cancer ten years ago."

"I'm sorry," Marina said softly. "Did she...?"

"She died," Morgan confirmed. "But she put up quite a fight. While she was in chemo, I played in a cancer charity tournament. I'd played in it before, but that was the first time it really meant something to me, you know? So, before the tournament, I bought a pink helmet. I needed a new one anyway, and, I don't know, I wanted to make a gesture for my mom."

"That's sweet," Marina said.

Morgan nodded. "She said it was silly, but I could tell that it made her happy. She came and watched me play… She survived long enough to see me play in three of those tournaments. Each time, I'd get a new piece of gear. For a while, part of me felt like… like throwing myself into that tournament every year was somehow helping. Like if I played hard enough, collected enough pink gear, won enough games, somehow it would help." She swallowed. "Obviously, it didn't. You can't cure cancer with helmets and trophies…" Morgan wiped a tear from her cheek. "After she died… You'd think I would have thrown it all away and never played that tournament again. But I didn't. I still play, and I never stopped picking up all things pink for hockey. I feel weird wearing pink in my day-to-day life, it's so 'girly,' and that's just not me. But at the rink I'm tough. I'm the best in my division. Nobody can make me feel like wearing pink makes me some stupid girl. It makes me strong. Like my mom was…"

"Oh, hun," Marina put her arms around Morgan, and Morgan leaned into her. It was mortifying to cry in front of others, but this was Marina. And somehow, allowing herself to be vulnerable felt *good*. As deeply as it hurt to think about her mother, Morgan was glad that she'd told the story.

"You must miss her so much," Marina said, rubbing her back.

"I do. Every day," Morgan whispered. She sniffed back the last of her tears. "I'm sorry for dumping that on you."

"There is absolutely nothing to be sorry about," Marina assured her. "Thank you for sharing. It means a lot that you were able to tell me that."

"I'm glad I told you… I just wish I weren't such an emotional mess today," Morgan said. "I'm not usually like this."

Marina squeezed her hand. "You're a person whose emotions run deep. When you care, you *really care*. You don't do anything halfway. Including feeling. It's one of the things that drew me to you in the first place."

Morgan couldn't disagree. "I'm glad that's a plus to you." She touched Marina's face. "Because my feelings for you run pretty damn deep."

"Ditto," Marina replied with a little smile. She was so sweet, so pretty. Morgan bent and kissed her.

"Would you like to come inside?" Morgan asked when their lips had parted.

"Yeah, I think I've got a little time," Marina replied coyly.

Morgan swept Marina up into her arms again, as she had the day she'd been injured. Marina squealed in surprise and clung to her neck as she carried her inside. Morgan wanted to carry her up to the bedroom. She desperately wanted to make love to Marina—something they hadn't quite gotten to yet. *Why haven't we?* Morgan assumed it was because of Marina's injury, but she honestly wasn't quite sure. Marina had never said anything or done anything to indicate that she was ready for sex. *Surely if she's feeling well enough for softball, she's well enough for other physical activities.* But Morgan didn't want to presume anything. So instead of carrying Marina upstairs, she brought her to the couch.

Morgan sat down carefully—Marina still in her arms—so that Marina ended up on her lap. As soon as they hit the sofa, Morgan began to kiss her. But Marina slid off her lap. Morgan was disappointed at first until she realized what Marina was doing. She repositioned herself so that her knees straddled Morgan's hips and sat back down into her lap. Morgan sighed happily as Marina kissed her long and hard, her arms around Morgan's neck.

Morgan put her hands on Marina's hips and pulled her in closer. Her fingers traced along the top of Marina's leggings, her fingertips lightly brushing Marina's warm skin. Heat and desire throbbed between her legs; she itched to touch Marina—run her hands up under her shirt, to feel more of her soft skin.

"God, I could kiss you forever," Marina whispered against her lips.

"Yes, please," Morgan replied. She pulled Marina down to lay together on the couch—Marina on her back and Morgan on her side, one arm under her and the other on Marina's hip. She looked down at the dark-haired beauty. "I love you," she said. She felt Marina tense. Morgan hadn't planned to say that; it had just slipped out. She suddenly panicked and put her mouth back over Marina's before she could answer, kissing her until the tension left Marina's body. She wasn't sure she was ready to hear whatever Marina might say back. It was still so early. They hadn't even slept together.

"Morgan, I…" Marina began, between kisses.

Morgan slipped her hand beneath Marina's shirt, running her fingers up along her smooth abdomen and brushing them across her sports bra-clad breast. Marina gasped. Morgan could feel her nipple harden through the fabric. Marina pulled at her, kissing her faster, deeper as Morgan pressed her palm against her small breast, kneading it. Marina spread her legs and pulled at Morgan's body, inviting one leg between hers.

Morgan shifted her body weight, rolling on top of Marina. "Am I crushing you?" she asked.

Marina shook her head and pulled Morgan's face down for another series of deep hungry kisses. Morgan's body ached; the pressure of Marina's leg between hers was deliciously teasing. Morgan knew she was wet—so wet she might soak right through her leggings. She wondered if Marina was as wet as she was. She wanted to touch her, to find out. But the physics of it didn't quite work out—not on that narrow couch, not with Marina pushing herself so hard against Morgan's body. Instead, Morgan buried her fingers in Marina's hair, twirling and pulling gently at her curls as they kissed.

"Morgan?" Marina said quietly, pulling away from the kiss.

"Yeah?" Morgan replied, sitting up on her elbow and looking down at Marina.

"I love you too," she said.

Morgan's heart was in her throat. *She loves me too.* Morgan could hardly breathe for the feelings welling inside of her. She rolled off Marina and wrapped both arms around her, pulling her into a tight embrace so that Marina wouldn't be able to see the tears in her eyes. *I really am overly emotional today*, Morgan thought. "I'm glad," she whispered. "Because I love you so much." Marina had been right. When she felt things, those feelings ran deep. And right now, she didn't know if she'd ever felt anything as profound as what she felt for this woman right here.

Marina snuggled into her shoulder. "I could lay like this forever," she said, hugging Morgan back.

"Me too," Morgan said. It was so comfortable. So perfect. The emotional marathon she'd gone through that day—from the anticipation and frustration of the game to the love and connection she felt with Marina after—must have taken more of a toll than she had realized because before she knew it, she was sound asleep.

Chapter 18
Marina

Marina couldn't figure out why she and Morgan—if they did really love one another—kept getting so close to sex without ever getting to it. All her ex-boyfriends had gotten her in bed repeatedly before saying anything about love. *I don't know very much about dating women. Maybe this is normal?* Marina knew she needed advice.

"Are you free for happy hour tomorrow?" Marina texted Jessica as she walked home. "Morgan and I are meeting at the bar for dinner, but I have a light afternoon at work, so I was wondering if you want to grab a drink first."

"Sure thing, lover," Jessica replied with a winking emoji.

"I just want to ask you some advice about dating a girl," Marina quickly added so that Jessica wouldn't get the wrong impression. "You know I'm dating Morgan, right?"

"Duh, the whole world knows. You two are so sweet you should open a candy store."

Marina let out a small huff of laughter. "Shut up. I'll see you there then?"

"See you there!"

Jessica was already sitting at the bar when Marina arrived. She threw back a shot and patted the seat next to her.

"Hey, sexy," she said in greeting.

"Hey, how's it going?" Marina said. "Pulltabs, huh?" Nodding toward the orange basket of spent gambling cards in front of Jessica.

"Oh yeah, I love hitting the cardboard crack," Jessica replied.

"Any luck?" Marina asked, saddling up at the bar beside her.

Jessica held up one short but meticulously manicured finger. "Just one left." She plucked up the last pull-tab and rubbed the card against her breast. "Come on, lucky lefty," she said before reaching over to rub it on Marina's chest as well. "Double lefty luck." She ripped open the tabs. "Damn." She threw it into the basket. "I guess today isn't my lucky day."

"Can't win 'em all," Marina said.

"Come on, let's toast to my misfortune." Jessica ordered two shots of tequila and handed one to Marina.

Shots weren't really Marina's thing, but she played along, throwing back the alcohol with a cough.

"So, how are things going with *Morgan*? How's the sex? Oh, God, with you two, it has got to be so steamy," Jessica gushed, setting down her shot glass and wiggling her eyebrows at Marina. When Marina didn't reply immediately, Jessica's expression grew concerned; she tilted her head and looked hard at Marina. "What's wrong?"

Marina looked down and fiddled with her fingers. She didn't know if sharing this with Jessica would be a breach of Morgan's trust, but at the same time, she wanted to tell *somebody*. "We... we haven't had sex yet."

Jessica sat back, eyes raised. "None? Like, at all?"

Marina shook her head. "Nothing other than kissing and cuddling... things got a little more heated the other night, on the sofa, but then it didn't go anywhere."

"What stopped it?" Jessica asked.

"I said something like, 'maybe we should go to bed,' meaning, you know... sex. But when we got upstairs, all we did was, like, go to sleep. Nothing I do seems to... progress the story, so to speak. It used to be so easy with Jason, but with Morgan..." Marina put her head in her hands. "I'm so confused."

"Have you just told her you want to fuck?" Jessica asked in her usual blunt manner.

Marina felt her face burn at the thought of saying something like that to Morgan. "Not exactly. But with Jason—"

"Forget about Jason." Jessica flicked her wrist as if brushing away a pesky fly. "He's a dude, a guy's guy, a *bro*." She rolled her eyes. "I'm sure with him, all you had to do was wear the right top or bend over in just the right way, and he'd jump up like a cat that heard the can opener."

"Something like that," Marina agreed, bobbing her head.

"Well, that's not going to work with Morgan. Not only is she a total chick, she's also very literal and straightforward, from what I've seen. And she's protective as *fuck* of you." Jessica drained her shot and tapped the bar for another.

"What do you mean, protective?" Marina asked, shaking her head when the bartender asked if she too wanted another.

"I mean, she defends you; she dotes on you. She doesn't want anybody to hurt you, not Liz or Kelly, and certainly not *her*. It *kills* her that she was the reason you got injured."

"But I'm healed. I'm fine. I told her it doesn't hurt, I—"

"That's not my point," Jessica sighed and put a hand over Marina's. "Answer me this: when you were dating Jason, did you ever do that thing chicks do where they complain about how their man is always in the mood? Like, did you ever insinuate that you only fucked him to shut him for *his* sake? Or say anything like, 'sometimes it feels like all he wants is sex?'" Jessica said in a breathy falsetto.

"Well, yeah," Marina said. "Probably."

Jessica squeezed her hand, nodding sagely. "Yeah, well, my guess is this: Morgan doesn't ever want you to talk about her like that."

"Huh?"

"She's fiercely protective. She is protecting you from herself. She's not going to do anything unless she is one-hundred percent sure that you really want to." Jessica raised an eyebrow at her. "*Do* you really want to?" she asked.

"Of course," Marina answered immediately.

"Then why haven't *you* initiated anything?" Jessica prodded. "You're acting like this is all on her, but I know you know it's not."

Marina didn't say anything. She knew Jessica was probably right, but that didn't make it easy to hear.

Jessica sighed. "Look, I know guys are easy, but you must have, like, *asked* for it some of the time, right?"

Maria bit her lip and nodded. She'd always hand a reasonably high libido. There were plenty of times where she'd gotten things going herself. But the thought of being that forward with Morgan was incredibly intimidating.

"So?" Jessica prodded again.

"I don't know. I guess I'm nervous," Marina admitted.

"What are you nervous about?" Jessica asked. "That she's going to turn you down?"

Marina shook her head. "No. I think I'm afraid I'll somehow do it wrong. I've never really done it like that with a girl before."

"What's there to do wrong? You got in my pants, didn't you? I'm a girl," Jessica reminded her.

"That was different," Marina protested. "That was just sex. And you knew how inexperienced I was. You knew *why* I was doing it. This is more than that… no offense."

"None taken." Jessica laughed. "So, you're worried about it affecting your relationship badly or something? What's the worst that could happen? Maybe she says she's not ready? I don't see that happening."

Marina ducked her head. "But what if we do have sex and it's… bad?"

"How could it be bad? You're a natural!" Jessica tittered.

"But we didn't… *I* didn't do… all the things."

"What do you mean 'all the things'?" Jessica laughed. "There isn't an 'all the things,' not in my book. There are so many ways to fuck. It would take a lifetime to hit them all with one partner."

"Yeah but, I… I feel like I don't even know if we had sex, you know, all the way." Marina was mortified to admit it but at the same time, who better to explain the ins and outs—so to speak—of girl sex than Jessica?

"We fucked, sweetie. I don't know what makes you doubt that," Jessica said.

"But I never went down on you," Marina blurted out. "Also," she added, ducking her head and lowering her voice. "I was never… inside you."

"But I was inside you," Jessica replied bluntly. "And I went down on you too. Plus, all the riding. Hun, we definitely had sex."

Marina must not have looked convinced because Jessica rolled her eyes and sighed like she was explaining introductory algebra to an engineer. "Think of it this way: if one dude fucked another dude right up the ass—as men are wont to do—is that not a real, complete fuck? Does it count as sex even if they don't flip the script and fuck the other way?"

"Of course it does," Marina said.

"I think you have your answer then. We had sex, darling—God, I sound like Cassie right now. Anyway, we fucked. If you are nervous about being the giver of those particular moves, that's understandable. But don't think for a second that what we did wasn't fucking. I fuck. I have a reputation to uphold, you know." She winked and kissed the air. "And it was fabulous. Didn't you think so?"

"Yes, it was. I'm sorry I—" Marina began.

"Oh, don't be sorry. Just tell me, do you want to fuck Morgan?" Jessica asked, plump lips pursed. "Do you really want to just *do* her?"

"Yes." Marina imagined being naked and rubbing on Morgan the way she had with Jessica, and her eyes rolled back in her head. "Yes, I want that so badly."

Jessica laughed. "Good. You've got me convinced. Now you just have to convince *her*."

"How can I convince her that I really want to?" Marina asked.

"Only one way," Jessica said with a smirk. "You're going to have to use your words. Be clear and upfront and ask for what you want. It's not that hard."

It sounded hard. But Jessica had a point. Morgan was protective, and she knew Marina was inexperienced. She was never going to be the one to push. Hell, the only reason they'd kissed the first time was because Marina had "used her words."

Marina sighed. "Okay… I'll give it a try…" She shook her head. "Why is this so hard? Why am I such a mess thinking about her? How is it that we can be so good together and yet leave me so unsure? Are all girl relationships like this?"

Jessica laughed out loud. "No. Cassie and I are *nothing* like you two. But I think we may be the rarity. We are unicorns, after all." She giggled and nudged Marina's shoulder. Marina giggled too. Jessica was one-of-a-kind.

"What's so funny?" The voice behind Marina's shoulder made her jump. She turned. Morgan was standing there, still dressed for work in a button-down shirt and grey pants, looking somewhere between bemused and suspicious.

"Oh, Morgan, I didn't—" Marina started before Jessica cut in.

"Morgan! So glad you're here! Your girl here is talking my ear off about you," she said, nudging Marina with her elbow.

"Is that so?" Morgan's eyebrows went up.

"She's so into you; she's making me miss my own tall drink of water." Jessica looked Morgan up and down with a mischievous little smirk. "Cassie's hotter than you, have I said that?"

"Jessica!" Marina smacked her on the arm.

Jessica giggled. "I'm just teasing. Morgan is so competitive; I just couldn't help myself."

"Well, Marina is hotter than you, so I guess we're even," Morgan said, grinning at Marina, who felt her face flush red.

"Oh, she is a sexy little lady; I won't argue there," Jessica said. "But we're so different. It's all about taste… speaking of," Jessica said in a suggestive tone. "Just wait until you taste *her*." She licked her lips, and Marina felt her blush deepen.

Morgan stared at Jessica, either uncomprehending or just too shocked to react—Marina couldn't tell.

"Jessica," Marina groaned, putting her hand over her face. "Sometimes, I swear you walked right out of a porno."

"And that's what you love about me." Jessica kissed her cheek. "Now, I'll just grab my check and get out of your way."

Marina shook her head. "It's on me. Thanks for the chat." She was grateful for Jessica's advice, but given the look on Morgan's face, she wanted to get rid of Jessica as soon as humanly possible. Marina owed her girlfriend some explanations.

"Thanks, lovely!" Jessica hopped off her barstool. "See you at the ballpark." With a flirty little wave of her fingers, Jessica strutted out of the bar.

"What the hell was all that about?" Morgan asked, taking Jessica's seat and giving Marina a stern look.

Marina wasn't sure exactly what to say. She didn't want to lie, but at the same time, she wasn't sure how Morgan would react if she told her that she'd called Jessica to get advice about their sex life. "I… uh…" she stammered. "I just met her here for a drink."

"Why?" Morgan's eyebrows knit together. "What was that bit about 'wait until you taste her?' Are you two still sleeping together?"

"What? No!" Marina grabbed Morgan's hand. "We're just friends, I swear. Morgan, you're the only one I—" She stopped. She'd almost said, "you're the only one I'm sleeping with." Only they hadn't really "slept together"—not in that way. That was the whole point of seeing Jessica, after all. Marina took a deep breath. "You're the only one I want to sleep with."

"Really?" Morgan asked, looking more skeptical than upset.

"Really," Marina repeated, nodding. "And I…" She took a breath and looked into Morgan's radiant face. *Use your words.* "I want to… you know, *sleep* with you. That's why I asked Jessica to meet me. I wanted to get her advice."

Morgan frowned. "You wanted *her* advice on *our* relationship? What did you tell her about us?"

"I told her that we hadn't slept together." Marina grimaced.

Morgan's eyes widened. "Why would you tell her that?"

"Because I didn't know what to do." Marina felt her throat tighten. "Because I was worried. I haven't dated a girl before. I didn't know if this was normal or if I'd done something wrong to make you not want to sleep with me."

"You didn't do anything wrong." Morgan sighed and touched her cheek. "I do want to sleep with you."

Marina let out a breath she didn't know she'd been holding.

"Did you think I didn't?" Morgan asked.

"Not exactly… I just wasn't sure why we hadn't."

"Why didn't you talk to me?" Morgan sounded hurt.

"I'm sorry. I should have," Marina looked back up at her girlfriend. "I was just feeling so… unsure. And I guess I thought that since I'd done those things with her, she would be able to tell me if I was doing something wrong."

"What did she tell you?" Morgan asked.

Marina smiled sardonically. "That I should talk to you about it."

"She was right," Morgan touched her cheek again.

"I know that now. And I'm sorry." Marina put her hand over Morgan's, pressing it against her face. "I love you, you know."

"I love you too." Morgan took her hand and kissed it.

"Was this our first fight as a couple?" Marina asked.

Morgan smiled. "I'd say more of a misunderstanding. But I'm glad we talked it out. I think we've both been feeling a little unsure in this area."

"You were unsure too?" Marina asked.

Morgan shrugged off the question. "It doesn't matter now. Because now that we've talked about it…" Her smile grew impish.

"We both know what we want," Marina finished.

"Exactly." Morgan leaned forward and kissed her. A shockwave of electric energy crackled through Marina's body. She wanted Morgan so damn bad.

"What are we still doing here then?" Marina asked, a little breathlessly.

Morgan grinned. "I have no idea."

The pair got from Main Street to Morgan's house in record time. Morgan's strides were significantly longer than Marina's, yet Morgan had to work to keep up with her. Marina was *motivated*. She didn't want to lose this momentum—she was too excited.

Once they reached the house, they practically sprinted up the stairs to the bedroom. The moment Marina's feet hit the shag carpet, Morgan pulled her in and kissed her deeply. Warmth spread through Marina's body as they kissed. She put her arms around Morgan's neck, undid Morgan's braid, and ran her fingers through Morgan's thick blonde hair. Morgan lifted Marina off her feet, and Marina wrapped her legs around her waist as Morgan carried her across the room to the bed. Morgan was so strong; the way she could carry her with such ease was incredibly sexy.

Morgan moved to set Marina down in bed, but Marina didn't let go, pulling Morgan down on top of her with a *whump* that made them both giggle. Morgan's undone hair fell freely around her face as she peered down at Marina. She looked so beautiful. The dim evening light highlighted her strong features and made her eyes a deep ocean blue. Marina wished she could somehow capture this moment forever.

"What are you looking at?" Morgan asked, a knowing grin on her radiant face.

"You, silly." Marina smiled back. "You're amazing."

"I know." Morgan winked at her. "You're lucky to have me. But I'll tell you a secret."

"What's that?" Marina asked.

Morgan grinned. "I'm even luckier," she said. "Because you are *beyond* amazing. You're a queen among peasants. And I should know, I dated my fair share of peasants. You are one of a kind."

Marina felt both flattered and a little envious. She never got to date a 'fair share' of women. But there was no woman in the world she'd rather be with than Morgan. The first woman who she had ever truly loved and who had ever loved her back.

"I love you," Marina said. "Now shut up and kiss me."

Morgan didn't need to be told twice. She kissed Marina hungrily. Heat and desire spread through Marina's body as they kissed. The need to feel Morgan's skin on hers was growing too strong to bear; she began to frantically unbutton Morgan's shirt. After what felt like an eternity, she was able to slip it from Morgan's shoulders. Under the shirt, Morgan was wearing a smooth white tank top. Without hesitation, Marina pulled it up and over Morgan's head. Morgan did the same with Marina's shirt, and they came back together in another series of passionate kisses. The warmth of Morgan's skin on hers was intoxicating. She ran her hands up and down along Morgan's back. Her fingers found the clasp of Morgan's bra and—with her hands shaking in anticipation—unhooked it.

Morgan sat up, legs straddling Marina's hips, and tossed the bra away. Marina froze, her breath caught in her throat. Morgan was so incredibly sexy—her breasts somehow the most mouthwateringly enticing things Marina had ever laid eyes on. She sat up and pulled Morgan toward her, putting her mouth over one taut pink nipple. Heat surged through Marina. *Is there anything more perfect in the world?* Marina didn't think she'd ever been as aroused by another person's body as she was by Morgan's—and the more she touched her, the hotter she got. Marina relished the sensation of Morgan's nipple against her tongue. As she licked and sucked, Morgan moaned encouragingly, her hips rocking against Marina's body.

After a moment, Morgan pulled Marina's head up off her breast and kissed her once. "You are far too clothed."

"Yeah?" Marina asked, breathless.

"Yeah." Morgan pulled Marina's tight sports bra up and over her head, causing Marina's hair to fall wildly around her face. Before Marina could even brush the curls away from her eyes, Morgan had moved back and was fumbling with Marina's belt. Marina put her hands over Morgan's, undoing it herself.

"Take yours off," Marina instructed. She let her head fall onto the pillow and then lifted her hips, pulling off her pants and panties at once. Morgan was quick at undressing; the second Marina kicked away her clothing, Morgan was on top of her again, kissing her— their naked bodies intertwined.

Their actions weren't as directed as things had been with Jessica; it was franticly passionate, wildly unpredictable. Marina felt dizzy with desire. She rolled on top, pushing herself against Morgan.

"I want you inside me," Morgan whispered in her ear, and Marina's heart rate doubled.

"I want that too," she replied. She'd never done it, but she knew she wanted to. Morgan took her hand and guided it between her legs. Marina gasped when she felt how wet Morgan was. "Oh, wow," she rasped. Her whole body seemed to tingle with anticipation as she ran her fingers along Morgan's entrance. Morgan rolled her hips, pushing Marina's fingers inside of her.

"Oh, my God," Marina whispered.

"Is this okay?" Morgan asked, pausing to look into Marina's face.

"Yes, oh God, yes," Marina assured her. "More than okay." There was nothing quite like being *inside* the woman she loved. She pushed her fingers deeper, and Morgan moaned. Marina rolled Morgan to her back and began to work her fingers in and out. Morgan's head fell back, and Marina couldn't help but smile. Then, quite without thinking, Marina slid her body down and put her mouth on Morgan, her tongue immediately finding her clit. She'd never tasted a woman before. She'd always wondered if she would like it. But she didn't just like it, she *loved* it. She didn't stop until Morgan came, shaking and moaning, and pulled Marina up from between her legs to kiss her.

"Oh, fuck," Morgan sighed contentedly. "You're good."

"Really?" Marina asked, skeptical.

"Really," Morgan assured her.

Marina smiled. "That's crazy, given that, you know, I'd never… um, done that before."

Morgan looked at her, eyebrows raised. "For real?" she asked. Marina nodded. Morgan pulled Marina into her arms. "Well, you're a natural, my dear." She kissed her.

"If you say so," Marina said.

"Mmm, I do. I'm quite impressed," Morgan trailed her fingers along Marina's skin. She kissed her again. Marina shivered; Morgan's touch was giving her goosebumps of excitement. Her whole body seemed to tremor with anticipation as Morgan's hand traced a path down between her legs. Morgan continued to kiss her as her fingers gently teased Marina. Soon Marina lost her ability to kiss Morgan back. It was all she could do just to breathe. *Oh, my God. Oh, my God.*

Morgan was talented. She played with Marina like a master violinist with a Stradivarius. Marina's whole body was on fire, alight with intense, focused sensation. Morgan brought Marina to the edge and back several times before leading her to one of the most intense orgasms Marina had ever experienced. She cried out, her head jumping off the pillow, her whole body shaking. She curled into a ball, and Morgan curled around her.

"You okay?" Morgan asked, a smile in her voice.

"Oh, fuck, yes," Marina squeaked as she worked to regain control of her breathing. She hugged Morgan's arm tight to her body. "How did you *do* that? That was like… magic."

Morgan laughed and kissed the back of Marina's neck. "Well, you know I like to be the best at everything I do," she said.

Marina snickered. "Well, congratulations, Morgan VanDolen. You win fingering."

"You laugh, but just wait until you see what I can do with my other parts," Morgan said. Marina turned to look at her. Morgan was grinning that big bright, beautiful grin of hers. She wiggled her eyebrows at Marina, and Marina laughed again.

"Okay," she said. "But not right now. Right now, I think I have to pass out for a while."

"Sounds good." Morgan snuggled up closer. "I love you, you know," she whispered.

"I love you too," Marina whispered back. This evening had not gone at all how Morgan had anticipated.

But her first time with Morgan had been so much better than she'd dared hope.

Would we have ended up here if we hadn't become friends first? Marina wondered. Somehow, she doubted it. Even if everything else in her life had gone the same way—sleeping with Jessica, then breaking up with Jason—Marina didn't think they could have ended up as a couple without being friends first. She wouldn't have trusted it.

Behind her, Morgan chuckled.

"What are you laughing at?" Marina asked, rolling over so that she faced Morgan.

Morgan pushed a stray curl from Marina's face. "You know, I'm not sure I would have stayed on the team if it weren't for you."

"Because you had a crush on me?" Marina asked.

"No, because you helped me get better," Morgan said. "I'm not a quitter by nature, but I don't know if I could have stuck it out without your encouragement."

"And that's funny?"

"Oh, no. I was just thinking about what you said, about me 'winning fingering.'" She laughed again. "I guess it's good that I'm better at sex than I am at softball."

Marina laughed out loud. "You can say that again," she teased.

"Hey now," Morgan said, narrowing her eyes.

Marina laughed again. "It's okay. We just have opposite expertise. I've been helping you get better at softball; now you can help me get better at girl sex."

"I hate to admit it, you know. But you're better at girl sex than I am at softball. At least from what I've seen." Morgan kissed her.

"Oh, trust me, I have a lot to learn," Marina said, kissing her back. "But if you'll practice with me…"

"Anytime," Morgan agreed.

Chapter 19

Morgan

The last game of the softball season came about far too quickly. With Marina back in action and Morgan keeping her attitude in check, the Dirt Bunnies were unstoppable. Well, not unstoppable in the winning sense, but certainly unstoppably happy. Morgan had apologized to Liz her next game back, and by the end of the season, they could hang out and have fun without incident. And now that Marina and Morgan were dating, Liz had finally accepted that Marina was queer after all. Morgan knew it still bothered Marina that it had taken her actively dating a woman to shut down Liz's skepticism. But she did admit that it had shut down some of her own self-doubts as well.

"Are you ready for today?" Marina asked Morgan as the two walked together to the ballpark.

"Ready for the game?"

"Ready for the last game," Marina clarified. "Ready to say, 'okay, VanDolen, this is your last chance to show them all,'" Marina said in a mocking imitation of her. Morgan shoved her lightly, and Marina laughed. "Seriously, though. Are you ready to make your final impression? To put an ending on your first season of softball?"

"I am. And you know why?" Morgan looked at her girlfriend.

"Why?"

"Because no matter how we do today, I'm proud of how far I've come." She grinned at Marina. "And I'm even more proud of my awesome coach and girlfriend."

"Are you proud of me, or proud that you have me?" Marina asked, her voice teasing.

"Can't I be both?" Morgan asked. "Because I am proud of you. You're a better player than everybody on that team, even when you were still limping around." This time Morgan imitated Marina—hobbling back and forth with comedic exaggeration.

"Oh, shut up." Marina shoved her back.

"But you're right. I am proud of myself for having the prettiest girlfriend to ever throw a ball." She winked at Marina. "I guess I win again."

"Maybe just focus on winning the softball game, alright, VanDolen?" Marina rolled her eyes.

"I think I'd rather focus on you," Morgan replied with a grin. "I'll play better that way."

Thinking about Marina made everything more enjoyable. It was the final game; she wanted to enjoy it. And it was against the Lions— the team with the hockey goalie who, at their last encounter, had made it abundantly clear that she hated Morgan. *I could have some fun with that too.*

"Go easy on me," Morgan said as she stepped up to the plate, behind which crouched the familiar goalie-catcher. "I'm just a hockey player, you know. This is your field."

The woman looked at her, glanced at her pink batting gloves, and smirked. "Alright, Pinkie Pie. We'll go easy on you."

Morgan squared up to the plate. She let the first pitch go by. But on the second, she swung with strength and control—as Marina had coached—and the ball flew past the short-stop and landed, bouncing, on the grass far back in the outfield. Morgan laughed the whole way to second base.

Kelly was up next. She hit a grounder on the first pitch that got Morgan to third base. Then Marina stepped up to bat. She was wearing the new rainbow tank top Morgan had bought her over a white sports bra, black leggings, and matching pink batting gloves. Morgan grinned. *Damn, my girlfriend is hot.*

"Bring me home, baby!" Morgan shouted from third base.

Marina turned and winked at her. "You got it, love."

The pitch almost seemed to move in slow-motion. Marina swung hard, hitting the ball with a crack. Morgan ran for home, but when she turned to see where the ball had gone, she stopped. There was no need to run. That ball was gone.

"Holy shit! That was a home run!" When Marina reached home plate, Morgan picked her up, spinning her in a circle before setting her down again.

"Yeah, I do those now and then," Marina said casually but with an impish smile.

Morgan pulled her in and kissed her. Then she turned at looked at the catcher. "Actually, I think it looks like this is my girlfriend's field," she said before turning and strutting back to the dugout. *Okay, so maybe I don't have the most sportsmanlike attitude.* She looked at

Marina, who was cracking up. But at least I still got the girl.

In the end, the Dirt Bunnies won by three runs. The team gathered in the parking lot for the last beers of the summer.

"Good game, everybody," Liz said, holding up her drink. "Here's to a great season. Thank you all for playing. I hope I see you back here next season. Go Bunnies!" The team cheered and drank.

"Will you be back next season, Morgan?" Kelly asked from across the group.

Morgan looked at Marina. "If my coach will keep helping me."

Marina snorted. "I suppose you aren't a total lost cause," she said, grinning.

Morgan turned back to Kelly. "I wouldn't miss it."